CRUEL

BRUTAL ACADEMY
BOOK 2

MAGGIE ALABASTER

JO BRADLEY

TRIGGER WARNINGS

Trigger warnings for mentions of sexual assault, attempted sexual assault, past psychological abuse, and human trafficking (not children).

CHAPTER 1

LILA

(10 years ago)

Every part of me trembled. My hands, my feet. My lips. Those most of all

"Please, Daddy…" I looked up at him. His face was like stone, cold and hard. Unyielding.

"I'll be good," I pleaded. "I promise."

He put a hand on my head. "This isn't about being good or bad, Lila. This is about you understanding what we do and why we do it. You're old enough to grasp the impact of the decisions we make. The more you under-stand, the better you'll be at making the right ones."

I lowered my gaze and eyed the thick, solid door. Made of some kind of metal, it didn't reflect a drop of light. If anything, it seemed to suck it in and keep it. I was careful not to touch it, in case I was sucked in too.

"I don't want to go in there, Daddy. It's dark in there."

In spite of his reassurance this wasn't about me being bad, I was absolutely sure I'd done something to deserve being put into a pitch black room by myself. Why else would he do it? What had I done? Specifically, what had he caught me doing?

My twin, Chloe, and I got up to all sorts of things, but Dad, he always told us to be careful getting caught. He made out that was the biggest crime of all. That and betraying him. Which I would never, ever do.

He laughed, but it was a bitter, humourless sound. "Of course it's dark in there, sweetie. That's the point. You'll go in there for a little while and understand the reason for these rooms down in the basement."

He ruffled my hair. "Nothing can hurt you in there." As if that somehow made everything all right.

Tears welled in the corners of my eyes. I blinked them away. Crying was a sign of weakness. If there was anything my father hated, it was weakness. Especially from one of his daughters. Even at the age of nine, I was well aware of the need to control myself.

Was that what this was about? Had I, at some point, done something that wasn't controlled enough? Had I cried? Laughed too loud? If it wasn't one of those, then *what was it? I worked hard at school. Chloe and I competed to be top of the class. We competed at everything. With each other and with other people. I beat her at most things, except making friends. She had loads of them wherever she went. I had a couple who stuck with me through everything. Everyone else thought I was stuck up bitch. I didn't care.*

Most of the time.

Not even when Chloe was invited to all the birthday parties and I wasn't. Or I was invited because people thought it was rude to invite her and not her twin. No one wanted me there, including me. I'd be the one hiding in the corner, waiting for the earliest opportunity to leave.

"In you go." Dad waved me inside.

I swallowed and looked down at the floor as I stepped inside.

It wasn't until the door clanged shut behind me that I let the tears slide down my cheeks.

The room was completely black. The only sound, the pounding of my pulse in my ears. I wanted to turn around and hammer my fists against the door, but no one would be able to hear me. That was the point. I was completely and utterly alone.

Instead, I sank down onto the floor and sat with my legs crossed.

"I'm sorry, Daddy," I whispered. Somehow, I'd figure out what I did wrong and I would never, ever do it again.

Lila

(Present day)

The truck ground to a stop, pressing all of us tight against each other. The woman beside me groaned. That was the only sound she'd made in the last few hours. That and dry retching. Her stomach must have been empty by now.

The smell of vomit was strong, sickening. It clung to the insides of my nostrils.

Thank fuck I didn't get motion sick. I was going to need all my strength to get the fuck out of here.

When I did, I was going to get my revenge on Chloe and whoever was working with her. Dane for sure. Zachary, probably. Someone else... I didn't know.

I'd spent hours thinking over the hours before I woke up here. I still couldn't remember the details. I had a cup of coffee in the Academy dining room. Everything after that... My mind was blank.

Muffled voices shouted from outside the truck. A gate clanged. The truck moved again, driving slowly over what sounded like gravel or dirt. The gate clanged closed.

The truck rumbled on for a minute or two, daylight flashing under the edges.

We passed over a bump. Several of the women groaned. More than one started to cry. I couldn't see any of them beyond vague shapes in the dim light. None sounded older than me. Of course not. Anyone that bought trafficked women wanted them young, pretty and undamaged.

I once overheard my father impress that on one of his employees.

"Customers don't want apples with bruises on them. Even one bruise reduces their value. If anyone leaves visible bruises, they can at best look forward to joining the girls on the auction block. At worst, a nice, slow death will serve as a sufficient deterrent to anyone else who thinks to touch my wares."

"Yes, sir." The man sounded both respectful and amused. "No... *Visible* bruises." He chuckled as though he said something hilarious.

The truck drew to a stop again. The front doors opened and closed, sounding like the driver and a passenger or two climbed out.

Their footsteps crunched around to the back. Metal ground against metal as the bolt holding the door locked was drawn aside.

I scrambled up to a sitting position and drew my legs in as tight as I could. I covered my bare breasts with my arms. As far as I could tell, no one touched me when I was unconscious, apart from removing my clothes. Nothing was painful or sticky. That wasn't a shitload of consolation. I was still naked in the back of a truck.

One, then the other door swung open on protesting hinges.

I raised my hand, blinked against the sudden glare of the late afternoon sun.

The light was a relief after the relentless darkness. A relief that lasted about five seconds before I glanced around.

I was packed in with about twenty other women. Most were around the same age as me. A couple were slightly younger and a couple slightly older. Three were blonde, one or two red. The rest had dark hair like me.

How long had my sister been planning this? Long enough, apparently.

A couple of men appeared in the doorway. One placed his fists on his hips.

"Good afternoon, ladies. You can call me Hades. Firstly, that's my name, and secondly, some of you will come to think of me as the worst kind of hell." His grin was a vicious slash across his face.

The man with him laughed. "He ain't wrong. Asshole is the worst motherfucker I know." He clapped Hades on the shoulder.

Hades laughed. "Listen to Brutus here. That's not his actual name. It's more of a description. Behave yourselves and you don't have to find out why."

Several of the women whimpered.

I bit my lip to keep myself from doing the same. More than anything else, I hated feeling vulnerable. I couldn't remember a time when I ever felt more so. Not even when I lay in the Academy hospital, with an oxygen mask over my face. Not even when my father put me in the basement room.

All of that was that was nothing to being naked in the back of a truck in front of people who intended to sell you to someone who wanted to use you as a fuck toy.

I had to get out of here before that happened. I couldn't assume Hunter and Parker would come for me. If they were, they would have stopped the truck hours ago. Or they'd be here right now, shooting Hades and Brutus, and making jokes.

And Slade— Where was he? Had he noticed I was missing yet?

No, right now I was on my own.

"If you treasure your pretty little skin, you will hop out of the truck and walk inside like we tell you to." Hades spoke as if the request was perfectly reasonable. As if somehow there was nothing wrong with what they were doing.

As if my father or someone like Reuben Brantley weren't paying them to do it. Did my father know where I was? Part of me would like to think he'd stop all of this if he did.

The realistic, cynical part of me remembered the last time I spoke to him. The way he blamed me for letting my guard down.

Maybe he thought I deserved this.

Maybe I did.

I wiped a tear from the corner of my eye before it could trickle down my cheek. Clearly I let my guard down again, somehow. I let my sister and her allies do this to me. If my father knew and approved, there was a chance no one was coming to stop any of this. That if I got away, I'd get no support from anyone.

I was completely, utterly alone.

The other women exchanged teary-eyed glances, but none moved. They were too terrified. Frozen to the pungent spot with fear.

I curled up in a smaller ball of misery. Even the dark, enclosed space that stank of sweat, urine and hours of fear, felt safer than stepping off the back of the truck. Here, it was harder for anyone to see me. To potentially recognise me. In the shadows, I was anonymous. I was no one. Just another piece of meat for the auction block.

If I wanted to move, my body wouldn't comply. I was paralysed in what little of the golden sunlight penetrated the back of the truck. Twilight was settling in. Soon night would fall. With night came more darkness. More terror, or perhaps a chance to escape this place.

As I finished that thought, one of the women jumped up. She leapt out of the truck, past Hades, and started to run.

Either he nor Brutus gave chase. Brutus looked dumbstruck, but Hades crossed his arms and looked amused.

"Looks like we get to have some fun after all," Hades remarked.

The woman reached the gate. She gripped the bottom of it and started to climb.

A moment later, she screamed and was thrown backwards. She landed on the gravel with a thud and a cry of pain.

"That's going to leave marks," Brutus remarked. "Stupid bitch."

"Mm-hmmm," Hades agreed. Over his shoulder, he addressed the rest of us. "You will have noticed the fence is electrified. It's currently on a lower setting. At night, it will be in a higher setting. We'd prefer you didn't damage your skin."

He turned around to face us. "There's worse if you don't cooperate."

Several of the women sobbed harder.

One by one, they started to climb out of the back of the truck, keeping close together. Several put their arms around each other, as though somehow that would keep them safe.

I was one of the last to slip down, trying to keep the trembling in my hands at bay. I didn't want to show fear, but suppressing it was difficult.

Brutus looked me up and down, but Hades only gave me a disinterested glance. He strode over to the woman who tried to escape, as she struggled to her feet. He stepped around her, appraising the grazes on her back.

He clicked his tongue. "They'll heal. You better hope they don't leave scars. You don't want to be bought by the kind of client who likes scars on his women."

He grabbed her hair and pulled over to a dam a few metres from the truck. She struggled against him, sobbing. His expression unchanged, he forced her to her knees and shoved her face into the water.

"In case anyone was wondering what happens if you disobey." He held her down for about ten seconds before yanking her back up again. She gasped for breath. Water poured down her face and dripped off her chin. She tried to jerk away from him again, but he shoved her head back under the water.

Her arms flailed, legs kicked out behind her. He held her down for another ten to fifteen seconds, before pulling her back out.

Once again, she gasped and sobbed, but she didn't fight him. She sat back on her knees and cried while the water trickled down her bare body.

"Are you going to fight me anymore, sweetheart?" Hades asked. When she didn't respond, he lowered her face back towards the pond.

"I'll behave," she squealed. "Please—" Her eyes were huge with absolute terror, and the certainty that, if her face went under again, he'd hold her there until she was dead.

He'd be in trouble with his employer if one of us died, but if we all obeyed after this, he'd probably think it was worth the risk.

If anything, Hades looked slightly disappointed she wasn't giving him the chance to kill her. He wouldn't be the first person to get pleasure out of killing people. Hunter, Parker and Slade all seemed to get enjoyment from it. Right now, I'd take some enjoyment from killing Hades and Brutus.

This woman, she was innocent as far as I knew.

11

Her only crime might be the same as mine—letting her guard down. Trusting the wrong person.

Hades shoved her away from him. "See you keep behaving. That goes for the rest of you too. You'll only be here for a few days before you're moved on to the auction house. From there—that's up to your buyer to decide." He grinned as if that wasn't completely fucked up.

"Brutus, get them inside. They all need a wash and something to eat. Our gentlemen clients don't want them to be skin and bones, do they?"

Brutus chuckled. "No, they don't. And neither do I." He turned his face and his gaze settled on me.

CHAPTER 2

LILA

The inside of the building was nothing more than a large shed. Foldout beds sat in lines along one side. Along the other were open-fronted shower cubicles. We could get clean, but our captors would see everything.

Clean shift dresses sat folded on the end of each bed. A welcome relief from the assumption they'd keep us naked the entire time.

With the promise of being able to cover myself, I hurried to one of the showers and turned on the water. I thought it would be ice cold, but it was actually warm. A few degrees cooler than I'd prefer, but better than freezing.

A spout sticking out of the shower wall delivered liquid soap to my hand. Another was for shampoo. I lathered myself and rinsed in about a minute and a half flat, all with Brutus watching me, his hand beside the telling bulge in his jeans.

I shuddered at the thought of him touching me, and turned the water off with a snap. I plucked a towel from a nearby shelf and dried myself faster than I ever had in my life.

His gaze still on me, I hurried over to one of the cots and scooped up the dress. I was shaking it out when I became aware of his presence behind me.

"What's the hurry?" he asked. He placed a finger in my shoulder blade before running it down my back and over my ass. "You look good like this. I bet you're a lot of fun."

I slipped the dress over my head and tugged it down into place. At the same time, I tried not to be too obvious about jerking away from him. Electrified fences and dams might be the least of the punishments they'd use on us if we pissed them off.

And nothing pissed off some men more than rejection.

I turned around to face him. "I don't know about that." According to my guys, I was a ton of fun, but he didn't need to know that. He was only a handful of years older than me, but if this was what he did for a living, he could fuck off.

He chuckled. He raised his hand and pressed two

fingers slightly to my cheek. He trailed them down my face and over my lips.

"There's one like you in every batch. Smart. Sassy. Clever enough to know what it takes to stay under the radar, but with enough spirit to be interesting. You try to act cool and calm, but when push comes to shove, you'll fight back." He leaned in to whisper in my ear. "I bet you squeal really pretty."

I swallowed. "I don't—"

He pressed his fingers to my lips. "Shhh. No need to say anything. We both know. You and I, we're alike. We're survivors. We don't let people push us around and tell us what to do, what to be and what to think. We grab life by the balls and live it."

He dropped his other hand to mine and pressed it against his semi-hard cock.

"If you look after my balls, I'll look after you."

I forced myself not to flinch. I wanted to jam my knee into his groin.

He rubbed himself against my hand, making himself harder.

"See, you're already a lot of fun. How about you get down on your knees—"

"Brutus," Hades snapped. "Stop toying with the merchandise and put the truck away." He gave me a look like it was all my fault.

Asshole.

Brutus grunted softly but let my hand go and stepped away. "Later, baby," he said. He gave me a wink before he sauntered away, back out of the barn. A couple of minutes later, the truck engine kicked over and rumbled away from the building, the engine so loud the walls shook.

Hades and a couple of other men watched over the women while they washed. Hades himself leaned against a wall, legs crossed at his ankles, eyes half closed, taking in everything.

One of the women, a petite blonde with a silver septum piercing, grabbed up a dress and started to pull it over her sweat-streaked body.

"No you don't," Hades snapped. He straightened up and stalked toward her.

"Get clean first. No point dirtying a perfectly clean dress." He grabbed the fabric and pulled it out of her hand.

She lunged for it, but he slapped his hand against her chest, holding her back.

"You can stay naked if you prefer," he said easily. "I don't give a shit. The dresses are only a courtesy, not a necessity." He shoved her back.

She bared her teeth.

"Want to play, do you?" Like he had with the first woman, he grabbed her hair. He pulled her over to a shower and turned the water on.

No steam rose from it. He'd shoved the woman under the flow that must have been frigid. She squealed and tried to jump out. He held her under.

"Wash," he barked. "The quicker you do it, the faster you can get out from under this fucking cold water." His sleeve was already drenched to his elbow. He disregarded it and held her still.

She hissed, either at him or with the cold. Maybe both. She soaped and washed faster than I had.

He let her go long enough to wash her hair before stepping away and drying his sleeve with a towel. He tossed it at her to dry herself after she turned the water off. It must have been freezing, because his skin was slightly blue. And the towel was more than slightly wet.

She eyed the shelf of dry towels but must have realised he wouldn't let her use one. Instead, she rubbed the damp towel over herself and scurried away to grab her dress and pull it on.

Seeming satisfied the rest of us were going to behave, Hades strode around the room like he owned the place. More than one set of eyes followed him, full of fear, hate and anger.

When he got to me, he stopped.

"Well, what do we have here?" His blonde hair was slicked back off his head. His blue eyes were as piercing as the twins'. As ruthless and determined.

Familiar somehow. If he worked for my father, I might have seen him before. Maybe I should tell him who I was. This could be nothing more than a case of mistaken identity. Even as I had that thought, I dismissed it. This was all deliberately planned. Right down to securing so many women who looked enough like me that if anyone was searching for a brown eyed brunette, they'd find over a dozen. That would make it harder for anyone to track me down.

I dipped my gaze to the tops of his cheeks, rather than looking him in the eye.

"I'm no one," I said.

He tipped back his head and laughed. "If you were anyone else here, I'd commend you for learning so quickly. All the other women in this room are no one. Bodies, mouths, pussies. There for the taking by whoever buys them. They'll go wherever they're taken and disappear. But you…"

He stepped around me, his eyes on me. "You're here because someone wants you to disappear."

"I don't know what you're talking about," I lied. How could he tell me from anyone else here? Unless he and Brutus picked me up from Brutham Academy. If that was the case, he might have an inkling of who I was. I didn't recognise any of the other women around me, but I didn't know everyone from the

Academy. For all I knew, I wasn't the only one. If that was the case, why had he zeroed in on me?

"Don't you?" He flicked half dry hair off my shoulder. "I think you know exactly what I'm talking about. Let me tell you a story. I knew someone once who had some trouble with his family. They pissed off the wrong people. It happens, am I right?"

He moved around in front of me. "Sometimes families prefer to dispense family members who don't toe the line." He drew his finger across his throat.

I hadn't noticed a scar across his neck until then. It looked as though someone tried to cut his throat, but failed.

Shame.

"But sometimes, families prefer to make their family members disappear in a different way. They like the idea of thinking their dear sibling is suffering. They get off thinking they'll be used until they're broken. The particularly sadistic ones like to see their family members later. To see how they have changed. How they've fallen apart. Because some families are —" He considered for a moment. "Fucked up."

"I guess so." I shrugged. That sounded like something Chloe would do. Hell, it sounded like something *I'd* do. When I got back to the Academy, it was exactly what I would do to her. If she thought this was the end, she was wrong.

"I see you know what I'm talking about," Hades concluded. "Why else would Lila Bell be in a place like this?" He smiled at my expression, clearly amused he'd caught me by surprise.

"I don't know who that is," I lied badly. My pulse was racing so fast I thought my heart might leap clear out of my chest. I half wished it would. At this rate, I'd need another shower to wash away a new layer of sweat.

His smile widened. "Yes you do. For the record, I don't work for your father. But a couple of people send you their best wishes." He looked thoughtful. "Or the opposite of best wishes. Worst curses?" He shrugged indifferently. "Close enough. Whatever they are, they come from Chloe, Dane, Zachary and… Slade Lincoln."

CHAPTER 3

PARKER

"Ow, fuck." I tried to roll over, but the chains gave me nowhere to go.

I forced my eyes open. The relative glare made me blink a couple of times.

The room was dimly lit, but bright compared to the darkness the assholes had kept us in for the last few days. Was it three days or four? Hell, it might be five or six for all I knew. Too fucking long.

"You here, Hunt?" My mouth was so dry my voice was little more than a croak. The last time my throat felt like this was after screaming my lungs out at one of Wolf Venom's concerts.

Hunter wasn't a fan of their music, but I secretly liked it. Or not so secretly, but I didn't flaunt it. I loved my twin, but he was always jealous of Zeke and his musical ability. Me, I long ago accepted the fact I had none, and happily left it to those who did. I had talent in other areas. My cock was probably bigger than Zeke's anyway.

"No, I'm lying on a beach in the Bahamas," Hunter said sarcastically. "That pounding in your head is because you drank too many cocktails by the pool last night."

"I wish. We should do that when we get out of here. I hear there's a nice little resort in—" I stopped as the sound of an approaching truck rattled the walls around us.

"I don't suppose someone is coming to…"

The truck rattled closer before roaring past, tyres crunching on gravel. It sent up a spray against the metal side of the building.

The sound of the big engine gradually faded away and disappeared.

"I'm guessing that would be no." I scrunched up my face and shook my head, trying to clear the last of the fog from my brain. I was getting really tired of being drugged. Everything hurt, but at least we were alive. More or less.

The chain left enough slack for me to sit up, albeit awkwardly, since my ankles were duct taped together.

"I can probably pull off your tape." Hunter's feet were right in front of my face.

Normally I'd complain about the smell, but there was a slight chance I didn't smell much better. Besides which, I was grateful they hadn't killed either of us yet. Nothing would suck more than lying here next to my twin's body. Except lying beside Lila's. Honestly, I wouldn't be too happy if it was Slade either. A guy couldn't help admiring his dedication to our girlfriend. That was something all three of us shared.

I started to tease the corner of the tape away and tugged it bit by bit, unwinding it until Hunter's ankles were free.

He groaned and shook them out.

"They were dedicated." I tossed the tape aside. "That was around four times. I personally only wind it three."

"Looks like you need to up your duct tape game," Hunter remarked.

I snorted a laugh. If nothing else would get us through, humour would. "I'd hate to have a duct tape game inferior to these assholes. I can't decide if I'm offended or not."

"Save your energy," Hunter suggested. "Move your ankles over here."

I shifted over and lay still while he worked the duct tape off from around my ankles.

"You know, you're right. This is some next level

tape work. It's almost like they knew what they were doing."

"You don't need to sound like you admire them quite so much." I pretended to pout. "They aren't *that* good."

He chuckled. "No, they're motherfuckers. Soon to be dead motherfuckers."

Blood rushed into my feet, both painful and a relief at the same time. Who knew how long they'd been like that? Too long. I rolled my ankles and waved them around in the air for a while, reducing the stiffness.

"Thanks, bro."

"Any time, bro." He threw the tape aside and sat up. "Given these guys are assholes, they don't seem to be idiots; they're going to have some idea when the drugs wear off."

"Are you suggesting we need to get the fuck out of here?" I asked, fully knowing the answer.

"Yes, Parker, I am," he replied.

"Hunter, I think that's an excellent idea." I glanced down at my wrists. The handcuffs were the same ones that were on there the last time I was awake. We already knew they weren't coming off, not without a fight. Or a key.

That left the other end. The chains were attached

to the wall by a bolt, but the wall looked less than sturdy.

Perfect.

I placed my feet against the base of the wall, raised my hands in front of me and pulled.

The wall groaned and buckled slightly.

I leaned forward and threw myself back with everything I had.

The bolt loosened.

I threw myself back again once, twice. The third time the bolt flew out of the wall, throwing me back onto my ass. I landed with a thud on the dirt floor. Thank fuck it wasn't concrete or I could have broken my tailbone.

I caught my breath for a minute or two then staggered to my feet. My wrists were still handcuffed tightly and I was trailing about a metre of chain, but this was a significant improvement in my circumstances.

"Good job, Park," Hunter waited for me to step aside and copied my amazing—if I may say so myself—example. He grunted hard with the exertion, but managed to pull his bolt out of the wall.

I didn't even mind that it took him one try fewer than it took me to get free. There was a time for envy and trying to one up each other, and then there was a time to be fucking glad to be standing.

"Excellent work, Hunt." I helped him to his feet. "I'm guessing the door is locked."

"I won't take that bet, because if I was an asshole, I'd lock us in," Hunter said. He stepped over to the door and tried the handle. An awkward manoeuvre at best with his wrists also handcuffed.

The door swung open.

"Fuck," Hunter grumbled. "I could have won if I'd taken that."

"You win by getting out of this shithole," I pointed out.

"That is very true." He nodded and carefully stepped out through the door.

I followed close behind after gathering up as much chain as I could and holding on to the bolt. It would suck to make it this far only to trip over. Especially if I needed my feet for running away.

"Does this place look familiar to you?" Hunter asked.

I squinted. "Vaguely. It looks a bit like one of the properties owned by..." I stopped and squinted around.

"Caleb," Hunter finished for me. "If he's in on this, he's dead meat."

"You won't hear any argument from me." I loved our second oldest brother as much as Hunter, but chaining us up was not all right. "Although, if I had to guess, I'd say this place isn't used very often. He might not even know anyone is here."

The grass was almost up to my waist. The trees and bushes were overgrown. So much so, the shed behind us was almost entirely obscured on three sides by bush. On the fourth side was a gravel road in a state of disrepair.

"It's no Toorak mansion, that's for sure," Hunter agreed. "Caleb wouldn't be seen dead in a place like this."

"Or alive." I stepped over to the track and peered one way, then the other. "I'm guessing that's the way out." I nodded the direction the truck went. Assuming it wasn't heading to some location deeper in the bush. Either way, we had to pick a direction and try.

"You were wrong about the door being locked," Hunter said thoughtfully.

"So were you," I pointed out.

He ignored me. "Let's go this way." He started walking in the direction I'd already suggested.

I rolled my eyes at his back, but followed regardless.

"Keep your eyes and ears open. If they—"

We both heard the rumble of an engine at the same time. We dove off the track and into the thick of the grass.

It wasn't until I was crouched down as low as I could get, that I remembered the existence of snakes. Right now, I couldn't bring myself to give too much of a shit. If a snake wanted to kill me, the fucker could get in line. The same went for any spiders of whatever else might be lurking around. Enough people wanted us dead, we didn't need animals as our enemies too.

An old SUV drove past slowly. They didn't even slow down when they reached the shed. They went on rolling down the track and disappeared behind the grass and gum trees.

"Let's keep going." Hunter rose, but made his way slowly through the bush, stepping carefully, moving slowly.

We walked parallel to the road. I kept half an eye out for cars and trucks, and the other half for snakes. Apart from the occasional rustle of sound, and cry from a magpie or some other bird, the place was silent.

"This gives me the creeps," Hunter said over his shoulder. "Give me a dirty, smelly city any day."

"You need to think bigger," I told him. "I'd rather be between Lila's legs than here or a city." For one thing, she smelled better and was better looking.

"If you're not careful, people are going to start to think you're the sensible twin," he teased.

"Fuck that," I shot back. "That's your domain. I'm the goofy, better looking, but surprisingly smart one. With the bigger cock." With all of that, who needed to be sensible? Not me. I was more than happy to leave that to him.

"I'll give you goofy." He looked back and grinned. "The rest… I think all the drugs they've given you have messed with your brain."

He'd turned back the way we were headed so I said, "Consider yourself flipped off." I didn't want him to miss out on that.

He chuckled in response. "Love you too, bro."

We walked in silence for a while, some unspoken sense that we must be close to the road. Or close to— Something. What the hell we'd do when we got there, I didn't know. We were us, we'd figure something out. We were nothing if not resourceful.

"What do you think she's doing right now?" Hunter asked after a few minutes.

"Judging by the position of the sun, she's in class," I replied. "Unless it's later than I think it is. In which case, she's probably naked and wet in the shower."

We both groaned at the mental image of our queen naked, water dripping down her glorious body. I almost felt her mouth around my cock. I heard sucking and moaning sounds from between her lips. Thinking about her made me hard, my balls tight and heavy. The things that woman could do with her mouth. There was no one in the world like her.

"I don't know what I want more right now, to eat her or to eat a hamburger," Hunter said wistfully. "I think it's a tie."

Yeah, I would have liked something to eat right about now too. I might even go as far as to prioritise food over Lila's pussy. I was that hungry.

Hunter held up a hand. "There's a bigger shed in front of us. And a dam if you're feeling thirsty enough."

I was that thirsty, to be honest. I stepped up behind him and peered over his shoulder.

"And a gate beyond that shed." I nodded forward. "Here's where you tell me we're going to have to wait until dark, aren't you?"

He glanced up towards the sky. "It should only be a couple of hours."

I sighed with annoyance, but sat back down amongst the bushes to wait.

CHAPTER 4

PARKER

"It's empty." I peered in through the grimy window. The windows had no curtains, enabling me to see all the way across to the window on the opposite side. The moon was high enough to illuminate the inside of the large shed.

"It looks like someone was here recently, but they're gone now." Foldout beds were stacked in a corner, alongside a pile of what looked like thin blankets and towels.

"Ah," Hunter replied. "No prizes for guessing what Caleb uses this for."

Our brother's favourite pastimes included smuggling. Whether it was people, drugs or guns, he had his hands in it. Heading up that side of the family operation let Reuben keep his hands clean. Clean of that, anyway. Reuben preferred to dirty his hands in other ways.

"What are the chances they keep a spare key in there?" I mused. "Or a sandwich?"

"Judging by the apparent lack of anyone around, it wouldn't hurt to try to find out," Hunter said. "Maybe we can find a chainsaw, or something to get these fucking cuffs off."

He stepped around to the door and turned the knob. The door swung open silently.

"They don't believe in locking things around here, do they?"

"I suspect they're more interested in keeping people in here, not out," I suggested. I followed him inside, stepping carefully over the concrete floor.

It only took us a minute or two to come to the same conclusion. The place was empty of tools, or food. I managed to take a drink from a tap that hung over an old sink, but I almost got as much on myself as I did in my mouth. It was worth it.

"That was a bust." Hunter scratched at his thigh as best he could with cuffed wrists. "We—"

A flash of headlights shone through one of the windows.

I immediately dropped into a crouch. Hunter was only a fraction of a second behind me.

"Fuck," he swore. "I don't think they saw us."

"I fucking hope not." I stayed down as the gates clanged open. "Do you think whoever was here has come back?"

"No idea."

We got that answer a moment later when a car rolled past. It continued down the track towards the shed we'd woken in.

Before I could even suggest we make a run for the gate, it clanged shut.

"They're going to come looking for us pretty fucking quickly." Hunter rose and hurried towards the door. "It's not going to take them long to realise we're missing."

I followed him out and we hurried towards the gate.

"If I know Caleb at all..." Hunter bent down to scoop up a handful of gravel and throw it towards the fence. The moment it touched, the fence seemed to sizzle. The rocks rained back on us.

I threw up my wrists to protect my face. "Fucking hell," I growled. "Caleb is very quickly becoming my least favourite brother."

"I'm sure if he knew we were here, he wouldn't have the fence turned on." Hunter didn't sound so convinced.

"We need to figure out how to turn it off," I said. "How the fuck did they turn it off when they came in just now?" I jerked my thumb in the direction the car went.

"Remote-control." Hunter shrugged.

"Then there needs to be somewhere for the signal to go," I reasoned. "Look for a box on the side of the gate."

"You look for a box," he said. "I'm going to keep an eye out for the car, or someone coming after us."

I nodded and knelt down to scoop up a decent sized rock. You never know when a rock might come in handy for smashing boxes or heads.

I stepped out onto the track and approached the gate carefully. I was out in the open here, vulnerable. I wasn't used to the sensation and I didn't like it. People were going to die for what they did to me and my brother. People who weren't us.

It didn't take long to find a small metal box beside the gate. A red light flashed in the centre every few seconds.

Gotcha.

That was the easy part. The hard part was trying to position the rock in my hands so I could smash it against the box without touching the fence or smashing the crap out of my fingers. On a scale of one to a hundred, all of that would suck.

"You've got this, Park," I told myself.

"Get it quickly," Hunter snapped. "It sounds like they've found out we're not there anymore."

"They shouldn't be surprised, their hospitality sucks." I drew my hands back and smashed the rock into the flashing light. I pulled them back quickly, before any electrical charges could surge through me and fry the fuck out of my pubic hairs. That part of my body was on fire a lot of the time, but I didn't want it to burn like that.

The light winked at me like a teasing son of a bitch, then went on blinking.

I growled under my breath and smashed the rock into it again and again.

Finally, the sound of electricity shutting off buzzed through the air.

I lowered the rock and stood panting for a moment.

"You know what would have been even better?" Hunter asked. "If the fucking gate opened."

I twisted my upper body around to glare at him. "Excuse me for not being a fucking miracle worker. We can climb the fence now. You're fucking welcome."

I flung the rock down onto the ground and stomped away off the road.

Hunter swore under his breath. "Hey, Park, look I—"

The rumble of a car engine in the deepening dark sounded impossibly loud.

"Get the hell back into the bushes," Hunter barked.

"What do you think I'm doing, dickhead?" I knew he was sorry for implying that I should be doing better somehow, but I wasn't ready to forgive him yet. He knew I would soon enough. We always bit at each other, but at the end of the day we were virtually inseparable. The Brantley twins against the world. Us, Lila and Slade.

"Whatever you're doing, do it quicker," Hunter snapped.

We dove back into the bushes as headlights swept towards us.

The car skidded to a stop in front of the gate. The doors swung open. A couple of figures stepped out, the lights on their watches turned on.

"They can't have gotten far," one of them said. Male, but with an unfamiliar voice.

"With any luck, a brown snake got them." Also male. Also unfamiliar. Neither was Dane or Zachary. Not surprisingly, neither were Caleb.

"Two against two," Hunter whispered in my ear. "I like those odds."

I rose just high enough to peer over the top of the

bush. If there was anyone else in the car, they were hiding, ducked down like us. I decided that was highly unlikely and my brother was right. The odds were even, even with handcuffs on. Even with heavy chains dangling from our wrists. With empty stomachs.

We were still Hunter and Parker Brantley. No one fucked with us.

Hunter whispered the plan quickly. I nodded before ducking down low while he snuck away.

I watched the lights flash as they searched for us, and counted in the back of my mind. We were going to have to time this perfectly. If we didn't, we were highly likely to be screwed. There was at least a one hundred percent chance these guys had guns.

I counted to about two hundred before I slowly crept forward toward the car.

I got into position and crouched still, watching and waiting.

Somewhere in the darkness, a tawny frogmouth called out. Once, twice, three times.

On the third, I rose and rushed forward, keeping low. I sprinted towards the closest guy and looped the chain around his neck. This would be much easier if my wrists weren't bound, but I managed to get it around and yank it tight.

At the same time, Hunter came running out of the

bush on the other side and looped his chain around the other guy's neck.

They both struggled, but we had size, surprise and desperation on our side. Not to mention no hesitation when it came to killing. Especially if it meant getting the fuck away from here.

I pulled the chain harder and harder, savouring the grunting and gurgling as my victim struggled to breathe. He let out a choked cough, before he finally sagged. When he fell to the ground, he took me with him, tangled in the chain and, tired from lack of food and being drugged, I lay there for a while until I was sure the stubborn prick had stopped breathing, stopped twitching.

Only then did I dare to breathe and lift the chain off over his head.

Hunter was on his knees behind the other guy, shaking him back and forth as though he could take his anger out on the man's corpse.

"I think he's dead, bro," I drawled.

"Just being sure." He lifted the chain and shoved the guy onto the ground. He fell into the dust with a thud. "Any guesses on the chance these assholes have keys?"

"If they don't, I'm going to resuscitate one of them so I can kill them again," I growled. I rolled my victim over, pulled a gun out of the front of his pants before rifling through his pockets.

They were empty.

"Nothing," I spat. Not even something useful like a packet of nuts. Yeah, it was getting more and more difficult to stop thinking about food.

"I may have something," Hunter said.

I pulled the watch off my guy's wrist and used the light to illuminate the ring full of keys in Hunter's hand.

"I have to admit, that looks promising." I crawled over on my knees and held out my wrists while he teased one key out from the others. After three or four different keys, one finally clicked and the hand-cuffs fell away from my wrists.

"I've never been so happy to get handcuffs off in my life." I shook out my wrists for a minute before taking the key and unlocking his.

"Yeah, that *does* feel better." He shook out his own wrists. "I think I might be cured of ever wanting handcuffs on me again. Unless they're covered in pink velvet or feathers."

I laughed softly. "Everything is better with velvet or feathers." Almost everything anyway.

"Let's go. Nice of them to leave us a ride." I nodded towards the car.

"We need to take care of them first," Hunter said. Always the voice of fucking reason. He was right though. Two dead bodies within view of the gate wouldn't go unnoticed if anyone came looking for them. They would, there was no doubt of that. Whatever was going on here was bigger than Hunter or me. That was saying something, because we're pretty big.

I brushed dust off my jeans and grabbed the legs of the closest asshole. He was heavy, but I managed to pull him into the bush and dump him there.

I lifted the watch to look at the faces of both assholes. "Anyone we know?"

"Nope," Hunter replied lightly. "I've never seen either of them before. Which is ironic, because no one is ever going to see them again." He grinned, but the expression was strained, tired.

"Let's see if these pricks have food in the car. Or money to buy some."

We started back towards the car, but froze as another set of headlights stopped on the other side of the gate.

"Fuck," I muttered. "What now?"

The doors opened and a couple of silhouettes stepped out and moved around into the glare of the headlights.

"Fancy meeting you two here."

CHAPTER 5

PARKER

I groaned.

"Asher fucking DiMarco," Hunter drawled. "What a surprise."

"Hey, Zeke." I waved at our brother through the fence. "What are you two doing here?"

It seemed like a strange place for a couple of members of the biggest rock band in the world to turn up. On the other hand, Zeke and Asher both grew up in the same world we did. Hell, Hunter and I have disposed of bodies for them and their band-mates. What else are little brothers for?

"We could ask you the same question." Zeke cocked his head at me. "Slade Lincoln got in touch with us."

"He noticed we were missing?" I pressed a hand to my chest. "I'm touched."

"He did, but he wasn't as worried about you as he is about Lila," Asher said. He rubbed a hand over the back of his neck. "If I had to guess, I'd say he doesn't give a shit about you. Would you agree with that, Zeke?"

Before Zeke could answer, Hunter interrupted.

"What do you mean he's worried about Lila? She should be at Brutham, with him."

"That's what he said." Zeke leaned his hip against the side of the car. "She went missing a couple of days ago. Slade had Kennedy Knight hack into the tracker on Lila's earring. Her last location was here before the tracker stopped transmitting. Asher and I happened to be closer than Slade, so he asked us to come here."

"But there's no one else—" The blood drained out of my face. "There were people here."

"That truck," Hunter growled. "It went straight past us. If she was on it…"

Asher stepped forward and pressed his head against the wires of the fence. Any other time, I would have found it hilarious if the fence was still electrified. Seeing the smart ass drummer flying back through the air would be funny as fuck.

Right now though, thinking about what might be happening to Lila, nothing was funny.

"Wild guess here, but people that come here don't usually do it with their consent," Asher said.

"We think Caleb uses this place to run his human trafficking operation," Hunter said, with barely contained rage.

"That tracks," Asher said. "That sounds like exactly the kind of shit Caleb would be involved in." He had no more reason to like our brother than I did right now. "Can you call him and ask him where the truck is headed?"

"I don't exactly have a phone on me." Hunter patted the sides of his jeans.

"I'll lend you mine," Zeke said. "I'd do it myself, but Caleb would want a favour in return for information like that."

"Caleb really is a special kind of asshole, isn't he?" Asher observed.

Zeke shrugged and pulled a phone out of his back pocket. "No more than any of my other brothers." He gave us both a dark look.

"Burned by a guy who makes a living singing," I said sarcastically.

"I could always not lend you my phone." Zeke started to put it back.

"No, we need it," I said quickly. "Also, Hunter and I are both armed so you can hand it over or we'll shoot you and take it."

"Whatever happened to asking nicely?" Asher asked. He glanced at the gate, his gaze up and down. "You might have to climb out and get it."

I gave an experimental tug on the gate, but it didn't budge. There was probably a remote-control in the car, but after smashing the box to turn off the electricity, I doubted it would work. Finding out would only waste valuable time. If Lila was on a truck, on her way to fuck knows where, we needed to hurry to catch up.

I grabbed hold of the fence and scrambled up and over the top, narrowly avoiding snagging my jeans on the barbed wire.

Hunter was right behind me. He all but snatched the phone out of Zeke's hand and stomped a few steps away. He smashed his finger down on the screen a few times before putting the phone to his ear.

While he waited for an answer, I peered into the back of the car.

"You didn't bring Abbie with you," I said, disappointed. "I would have loved the chance to say hello. That woman has some of the best tits—"

"I wouldn't finish that sentence if I were you." Asher's tone was pleasant, but menacing at the same time. He'd probably love an excuse to put a bullet in our brains. Honestly, the feeling was more or less mutual. He was a DiMarco and they were on my shit list right now. With Dane right at the very top.

"You guys promised Reuben you wouldn't kill us," I pointed out.

Asher smiled. "We don't need to kill you to make your life hell."

"What are you going to do, sing?" I grinned. "I've heard you sing. Hell is reasonably accurate." Like usual, I was using humour to cover my anxiety. Although, Asher's singing was pretty bad. There was a reason he was the drummer.

Asher flipped me off. "I'm starting to think Lila came here voluntarily after all. To get away from you."

Zeke grabbed the back of my shirt when I lunged at Asher.

"Don't fucking touch him," he growled. He shoved me hard against the side of the car and held me there. He leaned forward until his cheek was almost pressed against mine.

"In case you hadn't noticed, dickhead, we're on the same side here. I don't give a fuck about Lila Bell, but I care about women being trafficked and abused. And Slade is a friend of mine. If you keep being a fuckwit, we'll leave you here." He shoved me a little harder before he stepped away.

I straightened up and moved away from the car, like I wasn't bothered at all.

"So violent." I brushed dirt off the front of my clothes. "I don't suppose you have a sandwich with you." I shot a glance at Hunter. He looked frustrated, angry.

"What do you mean you don't know? It's your fucking job to know shit like this. You're in charge of these operations. Reuben would be pissed if he—" He shook his head. "Our girlfriend is on that truck. If anything happens to her…"

I heard— h*eard* Caleb's laughter through the phone. If he was right in front of me, he'd be missing his balls in three, two, one… I'd hand them to him before I dragged him over to the dam and held him and his Armani suit under until he stopped struggling.

The fact Zeke and Asher looked equally pissed was no consolation.

"Listen here, you motherfucker," Hunter growled. "I want the destination of the truck and I know you can get it for me. I'll wait." He listened with a scowl on his face. His expression hardened. He glanced over at me.

"Whatever he wants us to do in return for that information is going to suck," I observed.

"You won't get any sympathy from me," Zeke said.

"Me either," Asher said. He opened the front passenger door of the car, reached in and pulled out a sandwich. He bit into it and smiled at me.

"Did I mention I have a gun?" I asked.

The asshole smiled broader and went on eating. I should have killed him back in Perth. Or Melbourne. Or Sydney. Hell, there were a bunch of places I could have done it and didn't. That was what I got for being too nice.

"Yeah, yeah," Hunter was saying. "Whatever we have to do. Just get us that information." He was silent for a moment. "Fine, call me back on this number."

He pressed the screen and glared at the phone as if somehow it was in on some conspiracy against us.

"He said he doesn't know the specifics, because he leaves that to the asshole who works for him. There are several different places they could take Lila to be auctioned. They keep it random so the police can't figure it out and they don't tell Caleb until they get there. They know what will happen to them if they try to screw him over, but this way if the police go after Caleb, he can't give them a thing and they can't pin anything on him. The dickhead in charge will take the fall."

"That sounds like Caleb," Zeke said. "Did he say who the dickhead in question was?"

"Hades fucking Turner," Hunter growled. "His brother, Ares, is dating Lila's sister, Kennedy. He's an asshole, but Hades is a thousand times worse. If he touches Lila, I'll rip his bloody arms off."

"Get in line," I snarled. "Hades is a massive prick. I'm not at all surprised he runs this part of Caleb's operation. It's exactly the thing he'd get off on. Having power over other people, especially helpless women." Lila was far from helpless, but when it came to Hades, I hated to think of them in the same room, much less him holding her in the back of a disgusting truck with other women.

Hunter paced back and forward in front of the headlights. With the fence behind him, he looked like an angry, caged tiger. One with claws ready to tear people apart.

"Any idea which direction the truck went?" Zeke asked. He looked up and down the otherwise empty road. We were in the middle of nowhere. Kilometres away from anything. Of course we were. Caleb wouldn't run an operation like this in the middle of the suburbs. That was more Samuel Bell's style.

"None," I replied. "Hunter and I were chained up back from the road."

"Chained up?" Asher huffed a laugh.

"Yeah, in case anyone gives a shit, we were drugged and kidnapped." I glared at the drummer.

That made Asher laugh even more. "Wait until I tell Abbie that. She's going to find it hilarious." He pointed a finger at me. "Don't say you didn't deserve it. How many times have you kidnapped her? Twice?"

I shrugged. "Something like that, but no harm came to her."

"It doesn't seem like much harm came to you either," Zeke observed. "Excuse me if I don't give you any sympathy either. I'll save that for Lila and the other women in her company."

"Who kidnapped you anyway?" Asher asked. "Not that I care or anything."

"Funny you should ask, one of them was your brother, Dane. Helped by Zachary Sinclair and Chloe Bell." Otherwise known as a pack of assholes.

"How about that, Dane getting his hands dirty." Asher spoke lightly, but he looked disgusted. For once, we agreed on something. Had hell frozen over?

Zeke's phone rang. Not with a Wolf Venom tune as I would have suspected, but one from Blazing Violet. There was hope for Zeke after all.

Hunter answered before the first bar was done. "What?" He frowned as he listened. "Yep. Yeah. Okay. We know the place. Yeah, we know we owe you one for this. You know where to find us after we find Lila." He sounded like he wanted to tell Caleb to fuck off to hell, but for now we needed him. As long as we did, we'd play more or less nice.

He mashed his thumb down on the screen and handed the phone back to Zeke. "Let's get the fuck out of here. We need to get to her before—" He shook his head and didn't finish his sentence.

He didn't need to. We all knew what might happen if we didn't get there in time.

"I'll text the location to Slade," Zeke said. "He can meet us there."

I slipped into the back seat of the car and tried not to look like I was freaking out on the inside.

We're coming. Hang on a little while longer.

CHAPTER 6

LILA

The rocking of the truck made my stomach turn and twist. What made me even more nauseous was Hades' words tumbling around and around in my mind. I was naïve to consider trusting Chloe or Zachary, but Slade… Was he really working with my sister? Was I that bad at judging who I let into my heart? Into my bed?

The twins trusted him, and I trusted them more than I trusted myself. Had they misjudged that badly?

I didn't want to believe any of it. Once the seeds were sown, I couldn't get the thoughts out of my mind. To make it worse, I finally realised why Hades looked familiar. He worked for the Brantley family. I wasn't surprised to learn they were behind this. What

I couldn't figure out was how my sister was involved. I didn't doubt she was, but the fact she might be working with another Brantley against me and the twins, was new. Unless...

Unless Slade organised this on her behalf.

The thought he was in it that deep made my heart hurt. And made me want to stab him in his.

I shifted my position to try to get comfortable and lifted a hand to my ear. Hades had made us take all our jewellery off shortly after we arrived at the big shed. He and Brutus had thrown every piece into a machine that ground them all down to nothing. Tracking chip and all.

The girl with the septum piercing, Danica, had refused to remove hers. Hades had held her arms while Brutus laughed and tore it out so hard it bled. While Hades ground down the ring, Brutus grabbed her hair, forced her to her knees and undid the front of his jeans.

I stood and opened my mouth to protest, but Hades cut me a look.

"Unless you want to take her place? Maybe you'd prefer to suck my cock?" He grabbed his groin and grinned.

I backed down and turned away, but couldn't shut out the sound of her sobs. Those hadn't stopped for hours. She was only silent now because she was asleep.

I suspected she would have preferred if she was dead.

"How long?" the woman beside me whispered. What was her name? Mary. Her skin and hair were a shade or two darker than mine, but she was about the same age as me.

"How long what?" I whispered back, my tone more curt than I intended.

She licked her lips. "How long do you think it will be until we get…wherever they're taking us? It feels like we've been in here for hours."

"Yeah, it does." It was hot, dark and uncomfortable, but the hours in here would be better than what was coming after. What Brutus did to Danica was going to happen to all of us. We didn't talk about it. We didn't talk about much of anything, but we all knew.

I had no intention of letting anyone do anything to me without one hell of a fight, but I planned to get the fuck away before it came to that.

Whoever did this to me, I was done being a victim. I would escape, and when I did, I would find out exactly who was behind this and they'd pay dearly for it. Breaking them wouldn't be enough.

"Why does Hades treat you differently?" Mary surprised me by asking. "Are you someone famous?"

I choked back a laugh. "Infamous, more like it. But no, I'm no one special. He just… Singled me out." Better to pretend he planned to toy with me when he got the chance, than admit who I really was. If she'd heard of the Bells, she'd know my father had a hand in doing this to other women. In her mind, that may make me as bad as Hades and Brutus. As bad as Caleb Brantley.

She should think that, because I was thinking it myself. What had I done to stop this from happening to other women? Nothing, because I never gave it any thought. Not for a moment. My father did what he did to make us rich and powerful. I was so far removed from the consequences, I didn't consider there were any. Especially consequences that involved innocent women. These weren't hardened criminals or corrupt politicians who deserved to be fucked with. They were women going about their daily lives when they ended up here.

It went without saying that when I became the head of the Bell family, I would shut down any operations like this. I'd insist the twins make their family do the same. I wouldn't stand for it a moment longer. There were dozens of other ways to make money.

"Why did he single you out?" Mary pressed. "He seemed to know you somehow."

"He's probably seen lots of women like me over however the fuck long he's been involved in this," I said. "No doubt he chooses one in every batch. Brutus too."

The other asshole had his eyes on Danica every time I saw him. He'd do a lot worse to her if it wouldn't leave her more damaged than she already was. Honestly, it was Hades' presence that stopped him. Men like him only gave a shit to a certain extent.

Mary shuddered. "Brutus is horrible."

As if saying his name woke her up, Danica resumed sobbing softly in the corner.

"Do you think they'll find us in time?" Mary asked.

"Who?" I frowned at her.

"Our families. They must be looking for us. The police must be looking for us. This many of us going missing, they'll be looking everywhere." She looked heartbreakingly hopeful.

"Of course they will," I said with as much certainty as I could muster, considering I felt none at all. The twins were missing. Slade might be behind this. My sister certainly didn't give a shit. My father wouldn't be looking for me if he blamed me for letting my guard down. The rest of the Brantley family would be happy to be rid of me, especially if they made a lot of money from selling me. The only consolation there was that maybe they'd be inspired to do the same to Chloe. If she did this to me, then she deserved nothing less.

"They might be waiting for us at... Wherever they're taking us," I said with a shrug. "A whole bunch of cops, ready to arrest their asses. They can lock them away to rot."

"I hear the guys in prison don't take kindly to fellow inmates who do horrible things to women." Mary looked surprisingly pleased at the thought.

I have to admit, I didn't mind it myself. "I hope some big, ugly asshole makes Brutus his bitch."

Mary laughed softly. "That would serve him right. I bet she's not the first one he's done something like that to. But she might be the last."

"She's definitely not the first," I agreed. I didn't want to think too much about how many went before her. Mary was right, Danica should be the last.

"Any idea when they're taking us?" Mary asked. "Are there just... Places men go to... To buy women?"

"I don't know," I admitted. "I suppose there must be." My father never told me and I never asked. Part of me wished I had, but the knowledge wouldn't help me now anyway. Not unless I knew a way out.

"I've never—" Mary whispered. "You know, been with anyone."

I didn't know why she was telling me that until she added, "I was waiting for my first time to be special. Not... Forced." Her voice was choked with emotion.

"I don't think being raped gets any better even if you've fucked a bunch of times," I said, more coldly than I meant to sound.

"I didn't mean to suggest it was," she said quickly. "I just... I want to go home." She sniffed.

"We all do," I said gently. As gently as I was capable of anyway. "We will get out of this. Didn't we already agree the police would be waiting for us at the other end of this? Or our families."

Was there any chance the twins were looking for me? Was there even a chance Hades lied and Slade was looking for me too? Hell, I'd even cling to a kernel of hope that my father was looking for me. If I didn't hold on to that, I might consider giving up and that was something I wasn't going to do. I couldn't let despair get to me. If I did, it would cloud my judgement and force me to make mistakes.

I needed a clear head and rock solid determination. If I was going to fall apart, it would have to wait until later.

"Yes, we did agree on that," Mary said. "Do you think it's possible?"

She was clearly looking to me to keep her spirits up. If she only knew who I really was, she'd be looking in every direction but mine.

"Not only is it possible, it's probable," I lied. "Brutus and Hades and the other assholes should be pissing themselves right about now. And whoever they're working for. I hope they're enjoying their last moments of freedom. They're about to lose that."

Mary's teeth flashed white in the dim light. "I can't wait," she said breathlessly. "I hope we get to see the looks on their faces. That moment they realise how screwed they are."

"Yeah that would be... Good." It would be better than good if it ever actually happened, but what were the chances? Not as good as I would have liked them to be.

"What did you mean when you said you were infamous?" She brushed tangled hair off her forehead.

I suppressed a wince. I'd hoped she hadn't picked up on that and wouldn't ask.

"I just meant I'm good at getting into trouble," I said evasively. "I mean, I ended up here, didn't I? What happened to you? How did you get taken?" Anything to change the subject.

She sighed. "I went on a date with a guy I thought was nice and decent. I thought we had a nice time. He took me to dinner. It was nothing fancy. We talked about all sorts of things, you know? Work, family, shit like that. I guess he slipped something into my drink, because I woke up on the back of this truck."

"What a prick," I said. She struck me as the innocent, naïve type. Someone all too easy to take advantage of. The opposite of me, most of the time.

"He really was." She nodded. "What happened to you? How did you get here?"

"I think it was about the same thing." My brow furrowed in thought. "The last thing I remember was getting a coffee in the... My university coffee shop." If she didn't know about Brutham Academy, then I wasn't going to enlighten her. The rest of the world wasn't ready to know about the existence of such a fucked up place.

"The next thing I knew, I woke up here too. I guess the barista put something in my drink too."

"Shit," Mary said softly. "I'm so sorry. I'm guessing they did that to most of us, if not all of us. Why do men suck so much?"

"I've often wondered the same thing," I said. I couldn't even say 'not all men,' because fuck knows the twins did plenty of similar things. I knew for a fact they'd drugged Abbie at least once. Not for the same reason, but they did it.

"That's why women go to the toilet in pairs. Because too many men can't be trusted. When I get out of this, I'm never going on another date ever again."

"I'm sure you'll find someone nice," I assured her.

We had to get out of this shit first.

CHAPTER 7

LILA

The truck slowed to a stop. The rumble of a garage door echoed, the gears grinding it closed behind us. Steel hit concrete with a harsh, resounding clunk.

The truck rolled forward for another minute or two before coming to a full stop. The engine turned off, plunging us into silence.

Mary gripped my arm, trembling fingers pressing into my flesh. We sat like that, huddled together until the back of the truck swung open.

"This is it, ladies," Brutus said cheerfully. "Holiday is over. Time to get out and earn your keep."

Danica sobbed and shuffled away from him, but she had nowhere to go.

None of us did.

Brutus pulled out a gun and waved over several

men. They gathered around the back of the truck, each looking more shady as fuck than the last.

"Let's not have any trouble, ladies. Out you get." Brutus waved the gun at us before he stepped back to give us room.

Mary's grip tightened, her nails digging harder into my skin.

"Those aren't police," she whispered.

Brutus aimed the gun at her. "Anything you want to share with the class?"

She shook her head hastily, hair flying this way and that. "No." Her voice trembled as hard as she did.

"Good, then get the fuck out of the truck," he said with a vicious smile. He kept the gun on her until she let go of my arm and scurried out.

I sighed and followed. Instinctively, I kept my eyes down, looking for ways out, while giving the appearance of not making any trouble.

"Do I have to drag you out by your hair?" Brutus snarled as I stepped over near him.

I contained a flinch, but froze until I realised he wasn't addressing me.

A red-eyed Danica was staring back at him. Her cheeks were wet with tears. She didn't bother to wipe them away. She skirted over to the end of the truck, as far from Brutus as she could get, and climbed out.

"Shame, I would have enjoyed that." Brutus laughed. After a moment, the other men joined in.

I forced my eyes back down before I shot daggers at them. Now would not be a good time to provoke Brutus.

"This way ladies." He gestured with his gun.

A wave of panic threatened to wash over me. It lasted until I realised he wasn't referring to the elevator, but the concrete steps beside them. They led up, out of the parking garage.

Cold and dank, they were better than the confined space of an elevator car. Being stuck in one of those with Brutus was 'worst nightmare' material.

The men formed a loose semicircle around us, presumably in case we decided to run. Where they thought we'd go, I had no idea. As far as I could see, the only ways in and out were from the garage door, the elevator or the steps.

The concrete felt like ice under my bare feet, but I trudged up along with the other women. Mary stuck close by my side all the way.

"What is this place?" she whispered. "I was expecting an abandoned warehouse, but this feels…"

"Not abandoned?" I suggested. We were clearly in a city, but I could only guess at which one. If I had to, I'd bet on Melbourne. At this time of year, Brisbane would have been hotter. The two journeys in the truck were too long, too far for to only be in Sydney. Unless we were driving around in heavy city traffic. That didn't seem likely. The outer fringes of Melbourne were a much safer bet.

"Maybe they use this place a lot for... Things like this," she said. "We're not the first."

We were definitely *not* the first, but she was so sweet and naïve, it clearly hadn't occurred to her until now this operation was something ongoing. Something much bigger than any of us.

All I could say in response to that was, "No. We aren't." I glanced at her to suggest we should stop talking. I didn't want to draw the attention of Brutus or any of the others. If I was going to get out of this, I needed to stay under the radar.

Luckily, she got the message and fell silent.

We passed two landings before the stairs stopped at a third. The door was open. Hades stood in the doorway.

"It's good to see you again, girls," he said with a smile that was more menacing than warm. Especially when his gaze lingered on me. "Come with me."

I missed neither the innuendo nor the wink he directed at me. At any other time, and any other place and context, I would have responded with, "in your dreams." Here and now, I kept my mouth shut and followed as he moved out of the doorway and across a carpeted room.

Along one end of the room was a stage, approximately up to my waist. The rest of the room was filled with chairs, all of them currently empty. It didn't take a genius to figure out what this room was intended for. We'd be paraded on the stage for the viewing and bidding pleasure of those who would be seated comfortably.

Assholes.

"Step up to the stage and through the backstage," Hades directed. "There you'll find showers and a change of…clothes." He chuckled.

I started up the steps, hoping to find a door that led out. Or a window with a fire escape. Or…something.

The backstage area consisted of a long table which spanned the wall. Across the wall, several mirrors hung. Chairs sat in front of each, so people could sit and apply make-up. At the end of the room was another door that led into a bathroom. I made out several showers and a couple of toilets.

The top of the table was covered with piles of bras and panties, each lacy and sheer.

Change of clothes my ass. I should have guessed that was what he meant. Of course buyers would want to see what they were getting before they placed any bids.

I spied one heavy door that led out of the dressing room, but it appeared locked. I was going to have to wait and try to figure out a way to get the fuck out. I was patient. I could bide my time a little longer.

Wrinkling my nose, I chose a black bra and panty set that should fit and hurried into the relative safety of the shower. There were no doors, but none of the men followed us in. They must have felt secure that we had nowhere to go.

Like I had in the big shed, I showered in about a minute flat and dried myself on one of the towels that hung off hooks on the wall. I wriggled into the bra and G string and glanced at my reflection in a mirror that was quickly becoming steamed up.

Hunter and Parker would have loved what I was wearing. The lace was so sheer it was practically transparent. My pussy and nipples were clearly visible through the silk.

"That looks good on you." Hades looked me up and down and grinned. "There's hairdryers, hair-brushes and make-up over there." He waved in the direction of the long table. "Go and make yourself extra hot. And before you—" he directed the statement toward all of the women "—think that making yourselves look messy will mean that you avoid being sold, think again. Firstly, we'll make you wash it off. Secondly, the better you look, the better quality buyer you'll attract. Trust me, you don't want to attract the cheapskates. Unless you want to end up with someone like Brutus over there." He nodded towards the other guy.

Brutus flipped him off, but grinned. "I don't mind taking the leftovers. If they've got a pussy and like to cry, they're exactly my type." He leered at Danica.

She looked back at him with a devastated expression on her face. She was clearly terrified exactly that might happen.

I didn't blame her for being scared. Life with Brutus would be short and brutal.

"You're such a ladies man," Hades teased. He gave Brutus a nod before heading towards the doorway and back down the stairs.

"I really am, aren't I?" Brutus eyed Danica again. He laughed when she shrank away from him. "Where do you think you're going?" He stepped over towards her slowly, like a lion stalking his prey. "I might as well make you dirty before you get clean."

She whimpered. And again, when he grabbed her hair and pushed her down to her knees.

"Don't," Mary said, surprising me and herself.

"Leave her alone." She lunged towards him, hands in fists in front of her.

"Mouthy bitch." Brutus raised his gun and fired a single shot into Mary's stomach.

She staggered forward a few steps, her eyes wide with shock. Her hands clutched her middle, blood quickly coating her fingers. She dropped to her knees before collapsing to the floor with a soft thud.

The whole room froze.

Brutus laughed. He shoved Danica away so hard she fell on her shoulder with a cry of pain. She rolled over and scurried away to curl up beside the wall.

"You fucked that up, didn't you?" Brutus stood over Mary, gun held loosely in his hands. "You're ruined goods now, stupid bitch." He scowled like it was her fault, then shrugged.

His expression changed to a vicious smile that chilled my blood.

Would he really…

He knelt beside her. "Might as well have some fun."

He shoved her legs apart with his knees and shuffled forward between them. Grinning with anticipation, he pushed her dress up to her waist and undid his fly with one hand.

I didn't wait to see him pull out his cock. Without thinking, I grabbed one of the chairs and slammed it into his back as hard as I could. The impact jarred my hands.

He grunted with pain and slumped forward.

The moment he dropped it, I dove for his gun. My fingers closed over steel still warm from his hand. Acting on pure instinct, I found the trigger and fired off a shot into his head.

Then one each for the other two men who pulled out their weapons.

The women jumped to grab their guns and aim them on the other three men.

"You're not—" one of them started to say when Danica unloaded straight into his chest.

The other two raised their hands and dropped their guns to the floor.

What would Hunter and Parker do if they were faced with an unarmed enemy who surrendered?

I answered that question with a bullet in each of their brains. That was what they got for being involved in an operation like this.

I lowered the gun and dropped to my knees beside Mary.

"Holy shit," I whispered. This was beyond fucked up. My stomach rebelled, but I swallowed my last meal back down. I grabbed a fistful of fabric and tugged her dress back in place to give her some modesty.

"Mary?" She was so still, covered with so much blood. It soaked into the fabric of her dress and spread like a stain.

I'd never seen so much blood in my life. So much innocent fucking blood.

"We need to get her to hospital," one of the women spoke frantically.

I choked back my emotions and took a long moment.

"It's too late."

Brutus must have hit a vital organ for her to have died so quickly, but she was definitely gone. He would have raped a corpse.

I closed her eyes and wiped back tears. She deserved better than this. She should have gotten out of here with the rest of us. She would have met someone who treated her like a queen and had a long, happy life.

Now, none of that would happen. Not for her. It was so fucking unfair.

As for the rest of us... We needed to get out of here before anyone else came.

"Try the door." I nodded towards it.

Danica stepped over and rattled the knob. "It's locked." She aimed the gun at it, but quickly realised it was empty. She looked back at the man she killed with dawning horror on her face.

She'd killed him.

"Panic later," I snapped. I aimed at the lock and fired. The bullet tore through that and decimated a chunk of door.

"I don't know about you, but I'm ready to get the fuck out of here." I pushed the door open with my bare foot.

I froze.

"Slade."

CHAPTER 8

PARKER

"It's got to be around here somewhere." I glanced at the screen of Zeke's phone, then out at the street signs as we slowly drove past them. "Unless Caleb gave us the wrong address."

"If he did, it's the last thing he'll do," Hunter growled. "Zeke, pull over here. Let's take a look around."

"Whatever you say, bro," Zeke said with a hint of sarcasm. He pulled the car over to the side of the road and killed the engine.

Hunter was the first one out, but I was close behind. I half expected Zeke and Asher to drive away, but they got out too. I didn't kid myself that it had anything to do with Lila. It was the other women they cared about. Whatever. As long as our girl got out safe, sound and untouched.

They both slipped on caps and sunglasses, because nothing says 'famous person trying to go incognito' like an obvious disguise. Most people wouldn't give them a second glance if they just walked around like normal human beings.

I mean, being members of the biggest rock band in the world wasn't that big a deal, right?

I glanced back at the screen. "According to this, it's back there about fifty metres."

"Wait," Asher said suddenly.

"What the fuck for?" Hunter snarled.

The drummer nodded forward. "That. If we rush up there, we'll draw everyone's attention."

I squinted in the direction he indicated. Several men in Armani and Zegna suits were making their way toward a particular building, all walking like they owned the place.

Of course it wouldn't be everyday riffraff who wanted to buy women like Lila. Men like this wanted the best of the best. They'd pay well for it.

Assholes.

"Parker and I will go," Hunter said. "You two stand out like dog's balls." He glared at them as though daring them to disagree.

"You think no one will notice two dirty guys turning up at an event like this?" Zeke raised an eyebrow at Hunter. "If anyone stands out like dog's balls, it's you."

"Fuck," I said under my breath. "The last thing in the world I want to say is that Zeke is right, but…"

"Zeke is almost always right," Asher said. He gave my brother a fond look. They were so adorably cute together it was sickening.

"Thank you," Zeke told him. "I think. We'll talk about the 'almost always' later. In the meantime, let's find another way into the building. There has to be a back door."

I rubbed my forehead. It was starting to ache.

"It sucks when your big brother is right twice in as many minutes," Zeke said lightly.

"It's a new world record," I said sarcastically. I looked down at the map. "According to this, if we go down to the end of the street, around and back up again, we'll be at the back of that building."

I glanced back up and watched the businessman pass through the glass front doors. The place looked like some sort of underground gentlemen's club. That was likely exactly what it was. A place so exclusive it didn't need a sign. Potentially an establishment owned by the Brotherhood of Kings.

Even though Hunter and I were members, that wouldn't assure us that we'd be allowed to enter.

Sneaking around and breaking in it was then.

I handed the phone to Zeke and hurried up the street after him and Asher. A couple of people gave them funny looks, but most didn't look twice. None of them stopped to ask for autographs or selfies, which was just as well because we didn't have time for that shit and killing them in broad daylight wouldn't go unnoticed.

I resisted the urge to run, instead walking as quickly as I could while looking like I wasn't hurrying. Sneaking wouldn't work very well if we drew attention to ourselves.

"This is it," Hunter said as we reached the back of the building.

A driveway ended in a garage door, which was covered in an interesting variety of graffiti. From the look of it, it was painted recently, presumably to cover other graffiti. There was nothing more welcoming to a graffiti artist than a blank canvas. No doubt whoever owned the building painted it frequently.

Beside the driveway, a door led into the building. A surveillance camera kept watch on anyone who might approach.

At least, it did until I pulled out my gun and shot it.

The sound was loud enough to make me wince.

"Let's get inside before someone comes to investigate that." Hunter cut me a look that suggested he wished I hadn't done that.

I shrugged and tucked the gun away.

The door was locked, but when Hunter grabbed hold of the bottom of the garage door, it rolled up easily. He pushed it high enough for us to duck underneath and slip into the building.

We stood in a parking garage big enough for at least a hundred cars. Parked in the middle was a massive truck. The rear doors sat open.

I trotted over and peered inside. "It's empty, but it smells like... People."

Had Lila been in the back of that recently? She didn't like to let on, but I knew she hated enclosed spaces. They always made her shiver and her pupils dilate. From what I gathered, Samuel Bell didn't mind putting people in dark, enclosed spaces as some form of punishment. It wouldn't surprise me at all if he did that to her and Chloe. Shame he hadn't left Chloe and Zachary inside. Together or apart, it wouldn't matter. Dead was dead.

"She has to be around here somewhere," Hunter said.

I jumped as shots rang out from somewhere else in the building.

"That wasn't me," I said quickly, in case there was any doubt.

"No shit," Hunter said. His face was paler than usual, worry etched on his features. I didn't need any twin to twin telepathy to tell me what he was thinking.

Those gunshots might have meant we were too late. Worse than that, they might have seen us coming and decided to dispose of Lila before we got to her. If that happened, my heart was going to splinter into approximately seventeen billion pieces, each smaller than the last.

"There are—" Asher started to speak, but was interrupted by the garage door opening behind us.

Fuck. We all ran to hide behind the truck.

"The shots came from upstairs. If this has gone all pear-shaped, Caleb is going to be pissed."

I knew that voice. *Hades fucking Turner.* How many people did he have with him?

I chanced a glance around the side of the truck. Hades and four other men. No, three other men and a woman. So much for the sisterhood.

I stepped back and held up five fingers to the other guys. They all nodded and pulled out guns. Figured Zeke and Asher would be carrying too. You can take the boy out of our lifestyle, but you can't take our lifestyle out of the boy. They weren't in it as deep as us, but they couldn't escape it entirely.

Footsteps disappeared up the stairs, suggesting

Hades and his people went that way. If they went that way, so would we.

Typically, it was Zeke who took charge. He gestured for us to fall in behind him after taking off his hat and sunglasses and stashing them behind the truck's tyres.

Asher did the same before following close behind Zeke.

Hunter and I exchanged glances and nods, then we too were stepping towards the stairs and up as silently as we could go.

Shouting came from somewhere above us. A woman screamed.

We trotted up the stairs faster, keeping to the side to stay out of sight of anyone who might look back down. Every so often, I glanced up, gun ready to blow out brains.

"They went that way," someone shouted.

"Get after them," that was Hades.

At a signal from Zeke, we started to run. It was clear by now, no one was looking back. Their attention was all focussed ahead.

We bolted past a couple of landings, all the way to the third floor. A room full of chairs and a stage was empty.

"Backstage," Zeke said. He wasn't even puffing.

We slowed down and headed up the stairs onto the stage.

"This is more familiar," Asher remarked.

I rolled my eyes and resisted the temptation to shoot him in the back of the head just to shut him up. Only because I didn't want to waste a bullet.

We stepped into a dressing room. A woman's body lay on the floor. For a heart stopping moment, I thought she was Lila. Her hair was the same colour, the same length. There was so much fucking blood.

My brain finally registered that it wasn't Lila. I released a ragged breath.

Several men lay dead around the room. One had so many holes in his chest he looked like Swiss cheese.

"Anyone want to bet our girl was here?" I asked.

"Without doubt," Hunter said proudly.

"I'm guessing they went that way." I jerked my head toward an open door that also looked shot up.

"Let's go carefully," Zeke said. "If those women did this, the assholes might get desperate. We don't want them to shoot first and ask questions later."

"No, we fucking don't," Hunter agreed.

Guns raised in front of us, we stepped carefully through the doorway. It led to a long corridor lined with doors. At first glance, there was no sign of Hades and his people.

We walked silently across the worn linoleum floor. This section of the building wasn't meant to be seen by men in Armani suits. This was for staff. The doors must be offices or storage.

"Put your guns down," a male voice said from around the corner, just beyond the end of the corridor.

"You first."

I grinned. I knew that voice. Lila. Thank fuck she was alive. No doubt she was the one leading this escape. We were just here to help if necessary. The woman was a motherfucking badass.

"We have you pinned down in there." He sounded very confident. "We can wait here for reinforcements to arrive. You have nowhere to go. Put your guns down and no one will get hurt."

"We already have been hurt." That was a female voice I didn't recognise. She sounded distraught. Honestly, who could blame her? This whole situation was sixty-nine different kinds of fucked up.

"You can be hurt worse if you want," the man growled.

"Or you can fuck off," Lila replied. She sounded like she was past done with their bullshit. Honestly, she had a low tolerance level for bullshit in the first place. The last couple of days would have stretched her to the limit and beyond. She was going to need lots of chocolate, bubble bath, cuddles and orgasms after this. I knew just the three guys to give them to her. Especially me.

"I suggest you do what the woman says."

I frowned. That sounded like Slade. He must have gotten here right before we did. Evidently he hadn't bothered to wait for us.

Rude.

"Fuck this." Hades' minion sounded pissed off. "Let's just—"

Whatever he was going to suggest, he didn't get to finish.

Zeke flew around the corner. His movement was immediately followed by a shot, then another.

The three of us didn't hesitate to follow.

One minion lay dead outside a doorway. The other three turned their attention to us. There was no sign of Hades.

I got off a shot before one of the minions could shoot my older brother. Zeke, that was. Hunter was busy taking care of the other man.

Asher aimed at the woman but hesitated.

She didn't. She aimed at him and fired.

CHAPTER 9

PARKER

"Fuck!"

The bullet missed Asher by a hair.

I don't know who killed the woman in the end. Hunter, Zeke and I all fired on her at the same time. The impact of the bullets threw her back against the wall. She slid down slowly, leaving a trail of blood behind her.

I stepped forward carefully and peered into a room full of women. And Slade.

"Anyone else?" I asked with a grin.

"It's okay, he's with me," Lila said quickly to a blonde who aimed at me.

The other woman looked uncertain but lowered her gun.

"Don't worry, I only bite Lila." I put down my

own gun and stepped over to embrace her. "You look hot."

Her bra and panties were virtually transparent. If I wasn't hard from all the excitement, I was hard from looking at her.

She snorted at me and accepted Slade's T-shirt when he slipped it off and handed it to her. It fell to mid-thigh. Somehow it was even more adorable than transparent underwear.

Hunter shoved me aside so he could put his arms around Lila and give her a squeeze.

"It's good to see you. You too, Slade."

"Looks like we got here just in time." I scanned the room, smiling at the scared, anxious faces around me.

"We had things under control," Slade said evenly. As if he wasn't as happy to see us as Lila was. He could thank us later.

Lila glanced at him sideways. "You still haven't explained how you got here. How did you know where to find me?"

I knew that expression. That was the same one she had when she looked at her sister. Wary, mistrustful.

"The twins told me." Slade frowned. "What the fuck is going on?" He put out a hand to her, but she jerked away.

"The asshole running this operation, Hades, said you were working with my sister." Her voice was tight with stress and emotion.

He stared at her, open shock on his face. "Why the hell would I do that?" He lowered his hand and balled it into a fist. "Wait, did you say Hades? That explains it."

I slid the back of my knuckles down Lila's cheek. "I wouldn't believe a word that comes out of Hades' mouth."

"Absolutely not," Hunter agreed.

"My guess is Chloe told him to say that to fuck with your head," Slade said slowly. "I'll swear on anything you want me to swear on, I am *not* working with your sister. Or with Zachary. Or Dane for that matter."

"Wise man," Asher remarked. "I wouldn't work with him either." Neither he nor Zeke did more than glance at the half-naked women in the room. They also seemed to be oblivious to how many were staring at them in clear recognition.

Slade looked intently at Lila. "You believe me, right? I was trying to help you get out of here."

"They found us in this room pretty quickly," she said, still wary.

"They followed the sound of gunshots," Hunter said. "We were right behind them." He looked around the room, then back out in the corridor. "Where the hell is Hades?"

"Knowing him, he ran at the first sign of trouble," Slade said. "If there's anything he's good at, it's saving his own ass."

"To be fair, most of us are good at doing that," I said. "In the meantime, I don't know about you all, but I think we should get out of here. They did mention reinforcements."

"Yeah." Hunter nodded. "We need the quickest way out of this building."

"That's probably the way I came," Slade said. "I found a side door and ducked in while they were delivering crates of champagne. That led into the kitchen."

His words reminded my stomach I was starving. It grumbled but I ignored it. Food would have to wait until we were clear of this place.

"Lead the way." Zeke nodded to Slade. "You and Hunter at the head. Parker, Asher and I will go last. Women in the middle."

As usual, everyone jumped to do what Zeke said. Not literally, because that would be feeding his ego.

"You should have joined the army," I told him.

"You too," he replied. "They might have taught you and Hunter some discipline."

I flipped him off.

Asher grinned but didn't say anything, instead gesturing for the women to move ahead of us. He took off his shirt and offered it to the petite blonde who almost shot me. She took it gratefully and slipped it on.

Of course then the rest of us were obligated to do the same. A few of the girls wore white shift dresses, but the ones in underwear, with damp hair, were soon wearing oversized T-shirts.

Who said chivalry was dead?

Not that long ago, I would have been disappointed at all of those women covering up.

Today, I didn't care. If they needed modesty, then fine. I hadn't known where to look anyway. I couldn't really stare anyway. Not without Lila potentially shooting me in the balls. That wouldn't work well for me or her.

We hurried down the corridor and descended another set of stairs, this one as cold and dank as the one on the other side of the building. The smell of food reached my nostrils long before we passed the kitchen. I was sorely tempted to bolt in, grab some food and bolt back out again.

The word 'reinforcements' kept me in line.

Caleb was going to be pissed off enough that we'd killed his people without us having to kill more of them.

Not to mention I was *almost* certain he didn't want three of his brothers dead today.

Don't quote me on that though. Fuck only knows what goes through Caleb's mind. He liked to think he was suave and sophisticated, but without doubt, his thoughts were as firmly in the gutter as the rest of us. After all, he was trying to sell women here. Hunter and I have done some dubious things, but never anything *that* dubious.

"Here's the door," Slade was saying. He glanced back at Zeke.

Zeke nodded. "Everybody down. Open the door carefully. Parker, Asher, keep an eye out behind us."

"So bossy," I mumbled. In spite of that, I turned around and readied my gun, just in case.

Daylight and air rushed in as Slade opened the door.

I glanced over my shoulder.

He and Hunter weren't killed with a barrage of bullets. Lila stood right behind my twin, gun in her hand too. She was so fucking hot. Of course she'd made it through and brought all those women with her. If anyone could do it, it was her. She was beyond incredible.

I turned back in time to see an asshole in a suit walk around the corner behind us. I knew he was an asshole, because he was my brother Caleb. I won't lie, the temptation to shoot him then and there was strong.

He was surrounded by a couple of ridiculously burly bodyguards, who would definitely kill me if I killed him. Fuck that, I wasn't in the mood to die today.

"I see you found your girlfriend," he said smoothly. His eyes grazed all the women before settling on Lila.

"Your powers of observation are on point as always," Zeke remarked. "Observe this. We're leaving and we're taking these women with us." He was never impressed with Caleb's arrogance and posturing.

"I don't see any women," Caleb replied mildly. "None I know anything about. I'm merely here on business. What a surprise to run into all of you."

"See no evil, speak no evil." Zeke looked unimpressed. "Typical Caleb. You never were good at taking responsibility for anything you did."

Caleb raised an eyebrow. "You have no proof I have anything to do with this. If you walk out the door, I won't stop you."

"What, not going to offer us a share of the profits?" Asher said dryly.

Caleb raised his other eyebrow. "Would you take it?"

Asher barked a laugh. "Fuck no."

"Asher is trying to think up a reason not to put a bullet in your head," Zeke said.

"He's right," Asher agreed. "But we've wasted enough time here. These women have been through hell already."

I glanced back at Lila. She held her gun like she had the same internal conflict as Asher.

On one hand, Caleb had a part in what happened to her. On the other, killing Caleb might put the rest of the Brantley family offside and she may need them if we were ever going to form an alliance.

"If I was you, I'd look for things to smuggle that aren't people," I remarked. "I have a feeling it won't end well for you next time."

"Don't threaten me," Caleb said coldly. "I have connections you could only imagine. Several who would be more than happy to slice your throat while you sleep."

"Back at you," I told him. I wasn't going to be intimidated by him. "Can we go now?" I asked Zeke. "I've had enough of this family reunion for one day."

Zeke nodded. "Let's go." He gestured for Hunter and Slade to lead the way out the door, but kept his eye on Caleb the entire time. So did I.

I didn't trust that he'd let us walk away with hundreds and thousands of dollars worth of what he considered merchandise. The only reason for him to do it was because if he tried to stop us, that would be his admission of his involvement with the operation. He'd rather lose money than get his hands visibly dirty.

I had no doubt in my mind at some point he'd make us pay for this. When he did, I'd be ready. If Hunter didn't decide to strike out at him first. With any luck, he'd piss someone else off first. I more or less loved Caleb, kind of. I didn't really want to be the one who killed him. I doubted he shared the same sentiment about me.

I walked backwards, following the others while keeping an eye on Caleb's bodyguards. I couldn't tell what they thought of all of this. They were like a pair of stone walls, dressed in expensive black suits. No one would ever mistake them for what they were. Trained hitmen who worked as my brother's protectors. They wouldn't hesitate to kill if he told them to.

Lucky for everyone involved, especially me, he didn't. I stepped over the threshold and outside into the shade between buildings.

No one stopped us, but people passing paused to stare before hurrying on. It probably wasn't the first time they saw strange happenings here. It probably wouldn't be the last.

"My only regret is not being able to watch Caleb

explain to all those buyers that they're here for nothing," Asher remarked.

"You can go and watch if you like," Zeke said.

Asher grinned. "No thanks. My imagination is pretty good. Now, how are we going to get all of these women out of here?"

"If anyone suggests we go into the back of the truck, I will shoot their balls off," Lila growled.

"No one was going to suggest that," Slade assured her.

No one suggested calling the police either. Everyone was well aware Caleb was already telling all the men in suits to vacate the building. Or making up some excuse for being there. By the time the police arrived, the place would be cleaned up, dead bodies removed. Same with the sheds where we'd all been held. Even if the police believed what the women told them, they'd have no proof. Nothing they could pin on anyone. Apart from Hades, everyone involved in the operation was either dead or distancing themselves.

"I have an idea." Asher pulled out his phone, pressed the screen, and put it up to his ear. "Jackson—"

CHAPTER 10
LILA

"Nothing says subtle like a massive bus with Wolf Venom written down the side." I leaned back against Hunter and let him wrap his arms around me.

Hunter chuckled and nuzzled his face in my hair. "Sometimes being subtle is underrated."

"What would you know about being subtle?" Penn asked. The band's keyboardist glared at us. At the twins in particular. "You two are as subtle as a pimple on the end of a cock. Two pimples."

Parker laughed. "I see you still have your sense of humour intact."

Penn flipped him the bird.

The rest of the band was gathered near their manager, Jackson. Older than the rest of them by about a decade, I gathered he was also involved with Abbie. Three guys was plenty for me. I didn't know how she coped with seven. Unless they were all trained to put down the toilet seat.

"We also have another several of the tour cars coming," Jackson was saying to Slade. "We would have brought a rig truck, but Asher said no trucks." His denim blue eyes regarded the women before sliding over to me and the twins. The sides of his mouth pulled back slightly before he looked away from Hunter and Parker.

"Anyone would think they don't like us," Parker remarked.

"We don't," Penn told him. "You're a pair of assholes."

"What Penn said," Channing remarked. The band's saxophone player gave us a dark look, which was ironic given the things he got up to. Things, according to the twins, they'd helped him with.

"They're not worth it." Landon grabbed Channing's hand and pulled him over to where Abbie stood beside Zeke.

She was pretty, in spite of giving the twins the same look as all her guys did. Okay, in her case it was slightly understandable. They *had* kidnapped her. Twice. Up until now, I wasn't particularly sympathetic.

Now, I had some idea how it felt. Still, the twins were never going to do anything to her.

"Yes we are," Hunter said. "We're totally worth it."

Parker laughed and they exchanged high-fives.

"I see you two haven't grown up," Abbie told them.

"Nope," Parker agreed. "Still singing with these assholes?" He gestured around at the band and Jackson. "I bet you 'sing' really pretty."

The grin evaporated from his face when Penn lunged at him, and gripped him around the throat.

"You fucking little—"

Without thinking, I pulled away from Hunter, raised my gun and pressed it to the side of Penn's head.

"Get. Your. Hands. Off. Him," I growled.

In the corner of my eye, I saw Abbie pull out the gun Asher had at his hip. She aimed it at me, her blue eyes steel.

"Back the fuck off," she said coldly.

"You're not going to use that," Hunter told her.

"Don't count on it," Tully Cole, the band's lead guitarist, told him. His tone was cool and calm, almost amused. A trained assassin, not much ruffled his feathers.

"Zeke, don't make me threaten your girlfriend," Slade warned.

"Don't make me threaten *you*," Zeke replied.

"For love of..." Jackson sighed. "Everyone put your guns down. Have your pissing matches later. Right now, we need to focus on getting these women on the bus, in the cars and away from here."

Penn grunted something under his breath. "One more smart ass remark about Abbie and I'll break your nose again." He shoved Parker away and stalked off without even glancing back at me.

I looked at Abbie for a few long moments before we both lowered our guns. She handed hers back to Asher, but I kept hold of mine. The situation might have been deescalated for now, but the tension remained.

Parker rubbed at his throat. "You really would have killed Penn for me?"

I shrugged and stepped back into the circle of Hunter's arms. "No one gets to touch one of my guys like that."

If it was me, they wouldn't have hesitated to act either. Part of me was relieved I didn't need to kill anyone else. Yet.

Although—

"It was Penn who broke your nose?" For that, maybe I should put a bullet in his brain.

"Yeah, but it was no big deal," Parker said lightly. "Just a little misunderstanding."

"Nothing you didn't deserve," Penn said over his

shoulder. He opened the door of one of the tour vans as it pulled up behind the bus, and started to wave several of the women over to climb in. A couple of them didn't seem to have a clue who he was, but most of them stared. If he noticed, he gave no sign. It was just another day in the life of a guy like him. People looked at all of them wherever they went.

The women would have a story to tell when they got home. It wasn't every day they got rescued by rock stars.

"He's such a prick," Hunter said softly, unexpected emotion in his tone.

I turned around to look at him. He wasn't quite as outspoken as Parker, but he wasn't usually gentle either.

He gave me a faint smile. "I let you down. What happened to you never should have happened."

I shook my head. "I don't even know what happened to you and Parker."

"Chloe, Zachary and Dane happened," he replied. "Your dear stepbrother had someone at the Academy slip something into our drinks. The assholes had us chained up until we managed to escape. We stumbled upon Zeke and managed to find you here."

There was clearly more to the story than that, but that was all the explanation I was getting for now. Or maybe ever. I didn't suppose the details mattered all that much.

"That same someone drugged my coffee," I said darkly. "I woke up in the back of the truck."

He locked his eyes on mine. "Did any of them touch you?"

I shook my head slowly. "Someone stripped me, but that was as far as it went."

I couldn't know what they did to me while I was out, but I preferred to assume nothing happened. If it did, I might be better off not knowing. Seeing what Brutus did to Danica was bad enough.

Hunter growled in the back of his throat. "That was more than too far. When I find out who did that, I will fucking kill them."

"I believe you." I stood on my toes and kissed his mouth. "But you may need to get in line. The next person whose head I hold a gun to may not be as lucky as Penn."

Hunter grinned. "I love it when you threaten violence. It's so fucking hot." He kissed the tip of my nose.

"All right, that's everyone but you four," Jackson was saying. "I can have the driver take you back to the Academy on the tour bus, if that's where you want to go."

"We were hoping you'd drive us," Parker

told him.

"As tempting as that is," Jackson said sarcastically, "I have a tour to manage. As it is, you're lucky the guys and Abbie have a concert tomorrow night. Otherwise we wouldn't have been anywhere near here."

"I have my SUV," Slade said.

Parker grimaced. "Fuck. I was looking forward to travelling on that." He nodded towards the tour bus.

"You still can." Slade grinned.

"No deal," Jackson said firmly. "If you have alternative transport, you can take it. I'd prefer not to have the tour bus gallivanting all over the countryside."

"Has anyone ever told you you're a spoilsport?" Parker asked him.

"Of course not," Jackson said at the same time as Asher said, "Frequently."

Jackson turned around to raise an eyebrow at Asher.

Asher stuck his hands up to either side. "I know, I know. Drum machine."

Apparently that was some kind of private joke, because the rest of the band, and Abbie, laughed.

"Can we go?" I asked. A crowd was starting to gather around and stare at us. Of all the trafficked women, I was the last one. I didn't need people to gawk at me and wonder what I was doing standing on the street with a rock band. Especially since a couple of them, and Slade, were still shirtless.

"Of course we can, sweetheart," Hunter said. He slipped the gun out of my hand and put it away in the waistband of his jeans. "For safekeeping."

I nodded. "As long as you give it back if we see Hades." I wouldn't hesitate to use it on him if he showed up. I had a feeling he was long gone by now. If I was him, I'd be in another state already. I'd keep a very, very low-profile for a while.

"Definitely," Hunter agreed. "If I don't kill him before I have a chance to give it back. I can't guarantee what my instincts will do in that situation. I also can't guarantee I won't kill Caleb the next time I see him."

"If he and Reuben agreed to stop trafficking women, he can live," I said. "He might come in useful someday." Fuck knew what for, but I couldn't afford to alienate too many people, even if their last name was Brantley and they weren't the twins.

"Agreed," Zeke said. "I knew he got up to some shady shit, but this is not okay. If he did this to Abbie, I'd rip his head off with my bare hands." He exchanged looks with the twins and something passed between them. Like, suddenly they had something in common. A shared goal.

"If anyone is interested, I'm not too happy with my brother right now either," Asher said. "I knew he'd do a lot to get power, but I didn't think he'd stoop this low." He actually gave me an apologetic look. As if he had any more control over Dane than I did.

"That makes several of us," Hunter said. "He wanted power, but what he's got was some powerful enemies."

"Including Caleb," Zeke said. "There's no way he would have asked anyone to take Lila. He would have known it would end badly. There's a reasonable chance he had no idea until we told him. One of his subordinates was acting outside his orders. Working with Dane, Chloe and Zachary. I'll let you guess what that subordinate's chances are of living until the end of the year. Or week."

I exhaled softly. "It won't matter. Hades will pin everything on Brutus and he's dead. Anyone who could contradict Hades is probably dead too. Or they soon will be."

"Either way, Caleb prefers to use people than be used *by* people," Zeke said. "He may not shut this operation down forever, but he'll probably do it until he knows who was behind this. He'll want to avoid shit getting messy like this again."

"If there's anything Caleb hates, it's a mess,"

Hunter agreed. "But we will work on him to shut this down forever. There's plenty more shit he can get involved in."

He rubbed a weary hand over the back of his neck, reminding me he and Parker went through hell too.

"Maybe if we sit back for a little while, Caleb, Dane, Chloe and Zachary will take each other out," Parker said. He rubbed his hands together in gleeful anticipation of that possibility. If that was what happened, he'd be the first to suggest we bring popcorn and watch. Maybe a few beers and pizza.

"As awesome as that would be, that's too messy for Caleb," Hunter said. "He'll sit back and bide his time. Give them enough rope to hang themselves."

"Or he'll let Lila deal with them for him," Zeke said. He cocked his head at me. "Are you going back to Brutham?"

"Of course I am." I lifted my chin. "I'm not letting a little kidnapping and some human trafficking get in the way of my education." I didn't need to address the rest of what he said. We all knew I had every intention of dealing with them. I wasn't even close to broken, but by the time I was finished with them, they would be. Broken and begging for mercy.

CHAPTER 11

LILA

"Holy fucking hell," Parker groaned. "This is so good." He closed his eyes and bit into his fifth slice of pizza. "Pizza is always good, but when you haven't eaten in weeks, it's even better."

"It wasn't weeks," Hunter told him. He looked no less blissed out.

"Id elt ike id," Parker said, his mouth full. He chewed and swallowed before saying, "I said, it felt like it."

"That was what we thought you said," Slade said over his shoulder. "Are you making a mess back there?"

"Not yet." Hunter grinned. "So far, we're only eating food." He grinned at me before biting into his slice.

I smiled back and ate with only slightly less

enthusiasm than the twins. It wasn't very good pizza, but it was nicer than anything Hades and Brutus fed us.

Honestly, I only ate because I had to. All that killing and misery robbed me of my appetite. Remembering Mary and the way she died made my eyes sting. She was so sweet, so innocent. And me, who was far from being either of those things, survived. Some would say that was unfair. Others would say that was life.

I didn't know which was right. Maybe both, maybe neither.

"Are you all right?" Parker asked me.

"Yeah," I lied. "Just a little tired." I bit and chewed to avoid any more questions. For the moment anyway. I knew them better than to think they'd stop asking.

"You've all been through a lot," Slade said. "I feel as though…"

"None of this is your fault," I told him. "None of us knew Chloe had someone working for her, ready to drug drinks."

He said what I was thinking. "We should have anticipated it. Or better yet, beaten her to it."

"We didn't," I said. "But we're still standing. Imagine the look on her face when we step back into the halls of Brutham Academy. She's going to be livid her plan didn't work. Assuming she was working with Zachary and Dane."

"She definitely was," Hunter said. He glanced past me to Parker. Parker nodded.

"You should know, Chloe and Zachary are fucking. Dane was in on what happened to us, but fuck knows if he knows what their relationship is."

I wrinkled my nose. The last thing I wanted to imagine was my sister and my former stepbrother screwing each other's brains out.

"If Dane doesn't know, he should be told," I said.

"That's what we think," Hunter agreed. "We don't mind being the ones to tell him."

"I hope he doesn't know." Parker grinned. "Filling him in will be fucking awesome."

"With any luck, they'll tear each other apart." Hunter finished his slice of pizza and reached for another one.

"With even more luck, they'll take Chloe with them." I finished my own slice and licked my fingers.

"That would simplify matters," Slade said. He pulled the SUV to a stop at a red light. "It confirms what we all suspected though. Chloe was in on that teddy bear stunt."

"Chloe was in it balls deep," Parker said. "The bomb was some sort of decoy. Or a backup plan if the first one didn't get Lila. Or it might have been meant for Hunter and me. Either way, it wasn't meant to kill her. Zachary seemed smitten, from what we saw. But very much eating out of her hand. If she told him to curl up and suck his own cock, he'd do it."

I snorted a laugh and narrowly avoided choking on water when I opened the bottle to take a sip.

"Did you really ask Zachary to screw you?" Hunter asked. "That was the claim he made. Which we didn't believe, of course."

I grimaced and lowered the water bottle. "I might have been slightly... Pissed off when Chloe told me she fucked him. I mean, why her and not me?"

"That doesn't say much about his taste," Parker said. "I would have chosen you and only you."

"Of course you would," I told him. I wasn't naïve enough to think they wouldn't fuck my sister if I wasn't around. Before we were together, they'd fuck anyone who let them.

"Chloe led me to believe it was something magical and romantic between them. After Zachary and I screwed, she told me they were drinking and it just happened. I wondered if Zachary told her to make it out to be something special so I'd spread my legs for him."

Which was exactly what I did. I was young and dumb back then. I wouldn't fall for shit like that now. No, now it took a fake bomb to trick me.

Never again. There were only four people in this world I trusted and we were all in this car together, right now. Everyone else, I'd treat with suspicion. No one else would get close to me. Ever.

"I'm starting to dislike this Zachary asshole more and more." The light turned green and Slade moved the car away from the traffic light and toward the highway.

"Funny, I was just about to say the same thing," Parker remarked. "I've known some snakes in my time, but this dickhead is starting to piss me off."

"Bro, you're a long way behind if he's only *starting* to piss you off," Hunter told him. "He's been doing that to me for a while now. *Touch her and die* works in retrospect, right? Because the thought of him doing anything with you, makes me… I don't know, turn into a raging beast or something."

I patted his thigh. "The time will come that you can kill him if Dane doesn't do it first. I like the idea of you being a rage beast though. That's kinda hot."

"I'm a rage beast too," Parker said quickly. "I'm just the goofy rage beast."

"Yes you are," I told him. "You're *my* goofy rage beast."

"And you're my hero, because you would have shot Penn for me." Parker shoved the last of his pizza in his mouth and grinned.

"Do you think Abbie would have shot me if I shot him?" I didn't know her well, but she had a similar vibe to me. The kind that takes no shit from anyone. That explained how she dealt with seven boyfriends. Plus she had killed before to protect her guys. Only once, that I knew of, but that was all it took sometimes. Once you take that step, there's no going back.

"It would have been the last thing she did," Hunter growled. "And then killing her would be the last thing *I* did."

"And killing whoever killed you would be the last thing *I* did," Parker said. "And I wouldn't care because I don't want to live without either of you."

Slade cleared his throat.

"Or you," Parker said. "I think we can all agree we've grown attached to Slade too."

Slade looked up at the rear view mirror and grinned. "I've grown attached to you three too. When I realised all of you were missing..." His smile faded. "I don't think you've seen a raging beast until you saw what I would have done if anything bad happened to all of you."

"A few students would have failed?" Parker guessed.

Slade choked back a laugh. "That for starters. Things would get uglier and uglier from there."

"Has anyone offered you a drink?" I asked. The

twins both turned to look at me. "They went after the three of us. They weren't going to leave without going after Slade too."

"That's true," Hunter said slowly. "Unless…"

"I'm not involved in anything that happened to any of you," Slade said quickly. "I've already told Lila I—"

"I believe you," I said. "Either they swung and missed, or they were hoping we wouldn't trust you because they didn't do anything to you. In which case, they swung and missed there too."

"Interesting." Hunter nodded.

"It really is," Parker said.

I frowned. "What is?"

"The fact they apparently think we don't trust each other," Hunter explained. "That might be because they don't trust each other. They might assume we're like them."

"Oh." He was right. "If that's the case, we can use that to our advantage."

Hunter smiled slowly.

I knew that look. That meant he was up to something. Something I may or may not want to know the details of. Sometimes, I was better off not knowing, if only for plausible deniability. If I didn't know what they were doing, I couldn't stop them.

"Should I ask?" I cocked my head at him.

"Definitely not." He looked like the proverbial cat that got the cream. He usually did, but he was particularly smug right now. "There's only one thing you should do right now."

He shoved the pizza box onto the floor in front of us, grabbed my legs and swung me around until my back was pressed against Parker.

"You should enjoy yourself." He pushed up my oversized T-shirt and smiled at my sheer panties. "I'd prefer none, but I like these."

He parted my knees with his hands and leaned over to the full extent of the seatbelt to bury his face between my legs.

He pulled my panties aside and licked my pussy from bottom to top, then back down again. "You taste better than any pizza ever could." He kissed all around my pussy while tracing circles on my inner thigh with the pad of his thumb. He had me trembling in moments.

"I don't think I've been compared to pizza before," I said breathlessly.

"Favourably compared," he said. "Always favourably."

"Definitely." Parker gripped my chin and turned my face around just far enough to kiss me.

"You both realise how unfair this is," Slade grumbled. "I'm going to have to drive with a painful boner."

"Keep your eyes on the road," Parker told him. "I'm sure you had plenty of time with our girl while everyone thought we were off working for Reuben."

I remembered how he got me off on his desk while speaking to my father on the phone. My face and neck heated.

Hunter lifted his mouth from me and smiled. "Lila's blush says it all. I'm glad you were having fun while we were chained up."

He wasn't even being sarcastic. He was genuinely happy we were enjoying ourselves in spite of their absence and the reason for it. Of course, he wouldn't want me to go without orgasms. The twins were sweet that way.

"We have some time to make up for," Parker said. He pulled the T-shirt up further and slipped his hands into my sheer bra. He palmed and pinched my nipples while Hunter worked my clit into a shallow, quick orgasm followed by a deeper, longer one.

I felt as though I was floating above the earth, above the atmosphere. Somewhere out in space surrounded by stars. Weightless and tangled in bliss. A moment of precise perfection and pleasure. A place I would have liked to stay forever. Carefree and happy.

By the time I came back down from the second one, his face was shining, wet with my juices.

He sat up a little and licked his lips. "Best meal of the day. Of the year."

Parker slipped his hands out of my bra and pushed the T-shirt back down. "We have a long drive back to the Academy. Get some sleep. We'll keep an eye out for trouble."

"You should rest too." I tried to stifle a yawn but failed.

"We'll rest when we get back," Hunter said. "Right now, you need it more than we do. Don't stress, we'll be right here." He smiled and added, "I love you."

"I love you too." I nestled back against Parker and closed my eyes. I probably shouldn't sleep, but I was exhausted. That was the last thought I had before sleep claimed me.

CHAPTER 12

PARKER

"Home sweet home," I said as Slade pulled his SUV into a parking space and cut the engine. "Are you sure you want to do this?" I wound a thick strand of Lila's hair around my finger. I let it bounce free before winding another strand. Her hair was so soft, I could play with it all day. Currently it smelled like roses mixed with some kind of spice. Not her usual scents but compelling nonetheless.

"No, I'd rather spend the rest of my life in the back seat of this car," she said sarcastically.

Hunter grinned. "Funny, I was thinking the exact same thing." He twisted his upper body and pretended to crawl over to her.

She batted him away. "Save it until we're inside. I probably look like shit anyway." She sat up and looked at her reflection in the rearview mirror.

I clasped her shoulders and drew her back down. "You could never look like shit. Even if you looked like a potato, you'd still be gorgeous."

"Because the main ingredient of most of your favourite foods is the potato," she said. "If they added potato to pizza, you'd be in heaven."

"I'm not saying you're wrong about that," I said slowly, "But I am saying you're my favourite food, not the humble potato. Although, heaven would involve somehow adding beer to potato pizza."

When it came to actual food, I had relatively simple tastes. Especially compared to Reuben and Caleb. Joshua too. They were all born with a silver spoon up their asses and a taste for the finer things. Zeke, Lucas, Hunter and me, we preferred burgers to caviar. And beer to Bollinger. Although, I wouldn't say no to a glass of champagne most of the time.

Caleb, Reuben and Joshua would probably say it was because our mother didn't have the class as theirs. Since our father probably murdered their mother to marry ours, I'd never know.

Our family was nothing if not complicated. The only thing we knew for certain was that Zeke was conceived before our father's first wife died. If my father wanted someone out of the way, they were removed.

Until Dane and Asher's father removed him and

my mother. That was the main reason for the DiMarco family's downfall. They made a bid for power. They failed. Sucked to be them.

"That's disgusting." Lila wrinkled her nose.

"You say that now, but if someone invented it, you'd try it. You might even like it." I opened the door and stepped out before turning back and taking Lila's hand. I didn't want to let her out of my sight, much less let go of her physically. We were all going to have to be a lot more careful from now on. I thought we were before, but Chloe and her merry assholes proved us wrong.

For now.

"I'd settle for a long hot soak in the bath, a glass of wine and a platter of cheese, crackers and grapes." She sighed.

"We can organise two of those." Slade locked the car after us. "The only thing this place is missing are bathtubs in all the bathrooms. Or any of them."

"That was remiss of them." Hunter looked around slowly before leading us across the car park toward the Academy building.

"Remiss? That was downright neglectful," I said. "The school board should be ashamed of themselves. A person can get spanked, but can't have a long soak afterwards. What the absolute fuck?" I was only half joking.

"At least a person can get spanked." Slade's gaze slid over to Lila and he smiled.

"I knew you two were having fun without us." I sniffed. "I can't believe I missed a perfectly good spanking. It was good, right?"

Lila snorted the softest laugh. "It was definitely good. Don't worry, we can recreate it. Later. I'm sure Slade wouldn't mind spanking you."

Slade regarded us both, his eyebrows slightly elevated. "Is that what you want to see?" he asked her.

Her smile widened. "It might be." She clearly wasn't sure what, if anything, there might be between Slade and me or Hunter.

Honestly, I didn't know either. Right now, I felt like we were busy staying alive. That might have to be our priority at the moment. We had plenty of time to explore possibilities when we weren't dodging spiked drinks, assholes with guns and dickheads like Hades Turner.

"Let's get inside and worry about that later," Hunter said. "I don't like being out in the open like this. We don't know what might be waiting for us. Everyone be on alert."

He didn't need to tell us that, we all were anyway. So far, everything seemed normal. Music pumped out from the vicinity of the Academy bar. Voices shouted and laughed. They probably moaned as well, but I couldn't hear any of them.

Dozens of the windows, and the side of the building were lit. Windows sat open to let in the breeze, leaving the spaces inside protected by the not-quite-bullet-proof screens outside the not-quite-bullet-proof glass.

Apparently actual bullet-proof glass was both expensive and a safety hazard for people needing to get out of the building. Personally, I thought it was a corner the school board shouldn't have cut, like having baths, but I doubted they gave a fuck what I thought. Even Reuben and Samuel Bell, who both sat on the school board.

Hunter trotted up the steps in front of us and pushed the doors open.

Nothing exploded, imploded or collapsed. No one shot at us. The building didn't catch on fire. There wasn't even a stampede of man eating chickens, or fuck knows whatever else Chloe might think up.

"Okay." Hunter gestured for us to follow him before he stepped inside and hurried over to the staircase.

A few students gave us funny looks as they passed by, but no one seemed surprised to see us. They didn't even seem surprised us three guys weren't wearing shirts. Then again, we were us. Strange behaviour was kinda our thing. Hunter liked to refer to it as keeping them guessing, but whatever.

Either way, no one took any notice of us.

We walked up the stairs like we owned the place. Nothing to see here. No one was chained up. No one was trafficked. We just went out to do some stuff and now we were back. That was the impression we tried to convey. Whether or not we pulled it off was another matter.

I mean, of course we did. Totally.

We stopped outside Lila's door.

"Fuck," Hunter said softly. When we all turned to him in alarm, he added. "I don't have a key."

Slade grinned. "Thank fuck I do then." He separated one from the others on his keyring and slipped it into the lock.

"Do I want to know how you got that?" Lila asked.

He flashed her a grin. "Probably not. The fact is, I have one and this lock is being changed in the morning. Along with some other security measures."

She raised a hand to her ear. "Including a new earring with a tracker in it."

"And a clit ring?" I asked hopefully. "And cock piercings for Hunter and me. And Slade."

"I thought you loved me." Lila stepped into her room once Slade gave her the all clear.

"I do." I frowned at her.

"Then why would you want all three of your cocks out of commission at the same time?" She sniffed.

"We still have tongues," I pointed out. "And fingers."

"Personally, I'd prefer a nipple piercing," Hunter said. He closed and locked the door behind us. "Then Lila can have my cock all she wants while yours heal." He grinned.

"I've always wanted to get my ears pierced," I said. As curious as I was to know how a cock piercing felt, I didn't want to disappoint Lila. I especially didn't want to watch Hunter fuck her while I couldn't. That would suck in sixty-nine different ways.

"Let's worry about who is getting what pierced later." Slade inspected the window frames before pulling the curtains closed over them. "Everything seems safe here."

"Good." Hunter slipped into the bathroom and started the shower. "Queens first." He gave Lila a low bow and a cheeky grin. He pointed a finger at me as I was about to open my mouth. "You're not a queen."

"That depends on who you ask," I retorted. Still, I

was happy to help Lila out of her oversized T-shirt and into the steaming shower. I tugged off my jeans and followed her in. While she grabbed the body wash and started on the front of herself, I pumped shampoo onto my hand and washed her hair.

"Take a step back." I rinsed her hair, then applied conditioner and rubbed it in. I washed my hair and body quickly, then stepped out to let Hunter step in and rinse the conditioner out of Lila's hair.

Slade climbed in with them and ran his hands over her wet, shining breasts.

Both guys washed her legs, occasionally bumping hands until she was clean. While she languished under the water, they washed themselves. Shame, I was kinda hoping they'd wash each other.

By the time Hunter turned off the water, I was dry and holding out a towel to each of them.

"Thanks, bro." Instead of drying himself, Hunter turned to dry Lila. She raised her arms to let him rub the towel all over her, then handed him the dry one to use on himself.

While Slade and Hunter dried, I took Lila's hand and led her over to her bed. I lay her down, then lay over her, my weight on my knees and elbows.

"I missed you." I kissed her mouth slowly, careful not to push her too hard. After what she'd been through, I wasn't going to assume how ready she was for anything more than my tongue on her clit. If that was all she wanted, I was only too happy to oblige.

She surprised me by wrapping her legs around my waist. "I missed you too."

"I love your voice," I told her. It was so husky and hot. It never failed to make me hard, no matter what she was saying. She could read out a shopping list and my cock would pay attention.

"I love yours." She kissed me, her tongue sliding across my lips and pressing inside my mouth.

I wanted to devour her, starting with her tongue and working my way down from here. I wanted to touch every centimetre of her. I wanted to bury myself deep inside her.

"Leave some for us." The bed dipped as Hunter lay down on one side of us.

A moment later, Slade joined us on the other side. "Do you three mind if I…"

"You're one of us now," Hunter told him. "As long as it's all right with Lila."

Lila broke off our kiss. "It's more than all right with me. I want to be with all of you." She kissed me again.

Hunter slipped his hand between us and down to the top of her thighs.

She lowered her feet to the bed. I rolled to the side just enough to give him access to her clit.

"You're so wet for us," Hunter marvelled. He drew his hand back to let Slade feel how wet her pussy was.

"Very wet," Slade agreed. He rubbed his fingers over her clit in tiny circles. "So warm, wet and gorgeous."

Hunter slid his hand under Slade's and pressed a couple of fingers inside her.

"Mmm, that feels so…" Her words were lost in a moan and the rolling of her hips against both of their hands.

"Come for us," Hunter said softly. "Let us give you this."

"I… Mmm…"

She came, panting and moaning, the most beautiful singing I ever heard. Her back arched, breath fast. Just watching and listening almost made me lose my load then and there. She was a fucking goddess. One I fully intended to worship forever.

Finally, she flopped down against the mattress and lay still for a while, catching her breath until both guys pulled their hands from her delicious pussy.

I waited until she was ready and rolled us over

until she was straddling me. She looked down at me and smiled before she lowered herself onto my cock.

"Holy fuck." She always felt like the best kind of heaven.

Hunter opened the drawer beside the bed and pulled out a bottle of lube. He handed it to Slade.

"Only if you're sure?" Slade said to Lila, his head cocked to the side.

Her eyes were round. "God, yes please," she panted.

Under Hunter's gentle guidance, she leaned forward.

Slade slathered lube over her rear hole. He tossed the lube aside and stretched her slowly and carefully with a finger, then another.

"Please," she breathed.

He positioned himself behind her and slid inside her gradually, stopping every few moments to stretch her before he slid in all the way. The tip of his cock bumped into mine, separated only by a wall of muscle. An eloquent grunt slid from between the teacher's lips.

"So fucking good."

"Fuck yeah," I breathed. Sheathed in her warmth, while feeling Slade filling her ass was beyond bliss. I don't know what it was. There's no word for anything this incredible. It doesn't need one. This moment was just for us.

Hunter knelt beside her and slid his cock into her mouth.

I glanced over to see the same more-than-bliss expression I probably wore. We went through hell and we fucking survived. We deserved this moment for ourselves. This and more.

I looked back at Lila, her mouth full of cock.

"I love you," I told her.

Her smile around Hunter's dick was all the answer I needed. She loved me too.

Slade set the rhythm, thrusting into her and pushing her onto us. Over and over, slow as honey at midnight in the middle of winter, but warmer. Definitely that sweet though. Sweeter.

No one hurried. None of us wanted to. This could be our last night together. We needed to make it last as long as we could. To cherish every sensation.

Finally, Slade increased the rhythm. He drove us all harder and harder until one by one, we all came. Shattered apart into a million fragments before we came back together, sweating, but oh-so fucking satisfied.

CHAPTER 13

PARKER

"Hey, asshole," I said cheerfully. That wasn't the customary way to greet a teacher, even at Brutham, but in Dane DiMarco's case, it was appropriate.

He glanced up from his computer screen. A flicker of surprise crossed his face. He composed himself quickly. Not quickly enough, but he tried.

"Well, if it isn't the Brantley brats." He leaned back in his chair and laced his fingers behind his head. His resemblance to Asher was subtle. Where Asher was blonde, Dane had dark hair to match his soul. Asher got the smiles and personality, while Dane got the suspicious nature and asshole vibe.

"Not expecting to see us?" Hunter sat on the corner of Dane's desk. "I bet you weren't. Not until Chloe told you the time was right anyway."

I sat on the other corner. "Dude, you are the very definition of pussy whipped."

Dane laughed. "Pot, meet kettle. What are you doing here?"

"You were expecting us to be dead?" Hunter's tone was ice cold, dangerous. Even I was freaked out when he spoke like that. Crossing me was a bad idea. Crossing my brother was the closest thing to a death sentence a person could get without an actual bullet through their brain.

"Or chained up for a while longer?" I glanced over at my twin. "Maybe the plan was to auction us off too."

"Now there's an idea," Dane said slowly. "I'm sure we could find someone who needs a couple of boys who know how to dig."

It was my turn to laugh. "I didn't realise you were a comedian."

"I would have thought a pair of clowns would recognise one," Dane said dryly. "What do you want?

If he thought he'd insult us by calling us clowns, he'd have to think again. We'd been called a lot worse by better people than him.

"Did you know Chloe and Zachary were fucking each other?" Hunter asked bluntly. "Park and I had the…pleasure of hearing them while we were chained up."

"We'll be sending them the bill for our therapy," I said. "It's going to take a long time to get past hearing that." Spending the night lying under Chloe's bed while she and Dane fucked was bad enough.

"If anyone needs therapy it's—" Dane started.

"Most people," Hunter snapped. "There's nothing wrong with admitting you have issues. You didn't answer the question. Did you know about Chloe and Zachary?"

One side of Dane's mouth drew back. "Yes, I know. If you thought you could come here and stir up trouble by telling me that, you were wrong."

Hunter glanced at me. "Sounds like trouble in paradise to me." He looked back at Dane. "So you knew, but you're clearly not happy about it. Don't like sharing?"

"I'm not going to discuss this with you." Dane closed the lid of his laptop. "I'm sure you have enough problems of your own without coming here to bother me about mine."

"Not at all," Hunter said lightly. "We don't mind. Consider it a complimentary therapy session from us. Go ahead and vent." He gave Dane a 'give it to me' gesture with his fingers.

When Dane didn't speak, Hunter continued.

"Zachary is a prick and you don't want to share Chloe with him. Maybe you don't want to share with anyone else. But you want her and if that's the only way you'll have her..." He cocked his head at Dane. "Am I getting warmer?"

"Is there a point to this conversation?" Dane snapped. "Because, if there isn't, you can both fuck off. We'll be sure to do a more thorough job next time."

"Ouch," I said with a laugh. "I think he's threatening us, Hunt."

"Yeah, I got that vibe too, Park," Hunter agreed. He fixed his gaze on Dane. "Here's the thing. We don't like Zachary. We're pretty sure you don't like him either. I'm not entirely convinced his agenda is—how do I put it—Chloe-friendly. It's certainly not Lila-friendly. Do you think you can trust him or do you think he would shove both of them out of the way to take Samuel Bell's place if he got half a chance? Be honest with yourself if not with us, because we think we have a common enemy."

"If you think I'm working with you..." Dane scoffed.

"Fuck no," Hunter replied. "You're missing the point."

Dane looked at him coldly. "What is the point then?"

"The point is, neither of us wants Zachary to push Lila and Chloe out of the way. Parker, Slade and I are going to keep a close eye on Mr Zachary Sinclair. I suggest you do the same."

Hunter leaned in toward Dane. "Ask yourself this: Is there even the slightest chance Zachary would have let off that bomb in the vicinity of Chloe? I know that wasn't Chloe's plan, but can you be sure it wasn't his? Right now, I feel like we're living in an enormous spiderweb. Tangled as hell and sticky as fuck. We're going to look out for our woman. We have no doubt you plan to do the same thing. But remember something. Parker and I messed with her birth control. Zachary messed with a *bomb*. Who do you think is the greater threat?" He sat back.

"If you're not suggesting we work together then what?" Dane asked carefully.

"Just be on alert," Hunter said with a shrug. "No one will mind if you take out Zachary for overstepping. And he will. I'm willing to bet a big chunk of my trust fund he doesn't want to share with you. He might have a plan in place to get rid of you. Would you be all that surprised if he did?"

"I teach at Brutham Academy," Dane pointed out. "Nothing would surprise me less than a plot against me or anyone else. Hell, you two probably have a plan to get rid of me."

Hunter grinned. "Actually, we don't, but now you

mention it, maybe we should. What do you think, Park?"

"He *did* hold us down so Zachary could inject that shit into our veins," I said slowly. "But I'd turn my back on Dane faster than I'd turn it on Zachary. Or Chloe, to be honest. Given the way Dane's cousin Ric has managed to get in with Caleb, I'd think there was an opening if Dane wanted to take it."

"Exactly," Hunter agreed. "We don't have to be enemies. We don't have to work together either, but we could be... Is 'allies' too strong a word?"

"I think so," I said. "How about non-enemies? As in we basically leave each other alone. Although, Dane did threaten us a moment ago."

"I'm sure he was just surprised to see us alive and well. To be honest, I'm slightly surprised myself." Hunter placed his hand, palm down, on the desktop and leaned on it. "Killing us is a lot harder than it sounds."

"They say the same about cockroaches," Dane drawled. "The world will end, but there will still be cockroaches crawling the earth."

I grinned. "Yes, we are very resilient. Thank you for pointing that out. We're also smart. Smart enough to know who the real enemy is, and who should be neutralised, even if it means sleeping with the enemy. Not literally," I added quickly.

"We all knew you didn't mean it literally," Hunter said. He hopped down off Dane's desk. "I think we've taken up enough of your time. All we ask is that you think about what we said. If you don't, you're probably going to end up dead...pretty soon. That would be a shame." He started towards the door.

I slipped off the desk to follow.

Hunter stopped, his hand on the doorknob. He turned back to Dane, a sly look in his eyes.

"It would be a shame if you died before you saw Mina again."

Dane stiffened. "What are you talking about?" He placed his hands on the desk in front of him and pushed himself to his feet. "What do you know about my sister?"

"Oops," Hunter said as though he wasn't deliberately provocative. "You didn't know?"

"Know what?" Dane demanded. "Mina got married young and decided to stay away from this life." He didn't look entirely certain of that.

"Some of that is accurate," Hunter agreed. "But if you don't know, it's probably not my place to tell you." He started to twist the knob.

Dane lurched around the desk, and towards us. "What. Do. You. Know?"

"You should ask Asher." I had no guilt at all for

throwing Dane's younger brother under the proverbial bus. Better him than us.

"I'm asking you," Dane snapped. He looked like he was ready to grab both of us by the throat and strangle us simultaneously. It might be entertaining to see him try, however unlikely it was that he'd overpower both of us at the same time. Or individually.

"Where the *fuck* is she?"

I glanced at Hunter. He shrugged.

My gaze returned to Dane. "She's with Reuben," I said. "And when I say *with*—"

"Bullshit," Dane snapped. "She would never..."

"It's a long story and you didn't hear it from us," Hunter said. "I promise you, she's fine. Happy." He paused for a moment. "As happy as she can be. Reuben, Damien and Gianni take good care of her. Better than her fucking asshole husband did."

I grunted. If there was anyone who deserved a slow, painful death, it was Kurt Lasalle.

Dane shook his head. "You're full of shit."

"Like we said, ask Asher. He's seen her. We saw him see her." He was as impressed as Dane, but Hunter wasn't lying when he said our brother and his right-hand men were taking care of her. Helping her heal. I never would have guessed I'd be thinking that about Reuben, of all people. Even fuckers like him can surprise you once in a while.

Dane looked conflicted. He clearly didn't want to believe us, but chances were he'd be on the phone to Asher the moment we stepped out of his office. When he discovered we were telling the truth, he'd wonder what else we were telling the truth about.

My second favourite kind of fuck was a mind fuck.

"Get out," Dane said, his voice dangerously soft. "Stay the fuck away from me and Chloe. And anyone else in my family."

Hunter smirked. "That could be difficult, we're practically brothers-in-law."

"Get. The. Fuck. Out," Dane ground out. His face turned pink with fury. If he had a gun in his hand right now, he'd likely shoot our balls off. Lucky for all of us he didn't. I was, personally, very attached to my balls.

"All right, all right, we're going. Don't get your panties in a twist." Hunter opened the door and waved for me to step out first. He followed me out and closed the door behind us.

"That was a lot more fun than it should have been." He grinned.

"Messing around with Dane is always fun." I leaned over and pressed my ear to the door. Just as I suspected, it sounded like Dane was speaking to someone, his tone demanding. I couldn't make out the words, but the gist was clear enough. I almost felt sorry for Asher on the other end of the call. Almost, because if he got the chance, the drummer would probably kill us. And besides, he could have told Dane the truth ages ago. That was definitely not my problem or fault.

"She's what?" Dane roared.

"Come on, Park, our work here is done. This bit of it anyway. Now it's time to have even more fun."

I grinned. As much fun as it was to screw with Dane, there were other people it was more fun to screw around with. Figuratively speaking, of course.

CHAPTER 14

LILA

"Do I want to know what's going on?" I eyed my drink carefully, even though I'd watched Hunter open the can and check my glass carefully before pouring the contents in. He did the same with his beer. So did Parker and Slade.

"You'll know soon enough." Hunter toasted me with his glass and took a sip.

"I'm sure you'll be interested to know Gavin, who worked behind the bar, quit yesterday," Slade said. "He was also a barista."

"He had his fingers in a lot of drinks," Parker remarked. "Literally."

"I presume his income was supplemented by Chloe," I said.

"That's our suspicion," Hunter agreed. "We have some people looking for him. When we find him, we'll get some answers out of him." He sipped again and smiled.

"He's going to regret his life choices." I took a sip of my vodka, lemon and lime.

"He really is," Parker agreed.

Slade jerked his head towards the entrance. "Here we go."

Chloe and Zachary.

They both hesitated when they saw us. Flashes of surprise and confusion laced their exchanged glance.

Chloe set her lips in a firm, pale line and tossed her hair before stalking to the bar to get drinks.

Zachary hurried after her, speaking low in her ear.

"Interesting," Hunter drawled. "Either they weren't working with Hades, or he wasn't forthcoming about us all getting away alive."

"Not gonna lie, if I was him, I wouldn't have told them anything," Parker said. "That would lead to a one way trip to, you know, Hades."

He and Hunter high-fived.

Slade shook his head at them but smiled. "I agree, I wouldn't have told them either. Let Brutus take the blame. There's no reason for Hades to step forward and take it. He's an asshole, but he's not stupid."

"It would be a lot easier if he was," Parker pointed

out. His gaze was on Chloe and Zachary, clearly expecting something to go down.

"You're making me nervous," I told him.

He turned his face and gave me an apologetic grin. "You have no reason to be nervous. We have the situation well in hand. Right, Hunt, Slade?"

"Definitely," Hunter agreed.

Slade sat back and nodded. "Let's just say I'm glad I'm not on the opposite side to these two." He jerked his head towards the twins. "They don't get called evil for nothing."

Both of the twins grinned.

"Exactly, but this will top off all of that," Hunter said.

I glanced over as Chloe and Zachary settled on the couch on the other side of the room. She crossed her knees and leaned against the arm like she owned the place.

I wanted to scratch her eyes out.

"We should ask them to join our next Kink or Drink," Parker remarked. "Them and Dane. It would be fun to see the expression on their faces when one of them paddles Chloe while the other has to watch."

Hunter chuckled. "That would be fun, but this is going to be more fun." He rubbed his hands together and smiled like a cartoon villain.

"And we have front row seats," Parker added.

I turned back to my sister and former stepbrother as his phone rang. He pulled it out of his pocket and scowled the screen before pressing the device to his ear.

Whatever the person on the other end said, it quickly had him agitated. He gestured with his other hand while he spoke and listened.

Chloe put a hand on his arm and looked concerned. He shook his head and hung up the call. He said something to her as he tucked his phone back into the pocket of his jeans. She didn't look happy about it, but she lowered her hand and sat back.

Zachary leaned over to kiss her cheek, then rose and hurried out of the bar.

I frowned. "Is that what we're waiting for?"

"Nope, it gets better," Hunter said. "Keep watching, but don't look too much like you're watching. We don't want her to think we're up to something."

"We *are* up to something," Parker said.

"Of course we are, but we don't want her to know that." Hunter downed a gulp of beer.

"Right, play it cool." Slade sipped his own beer and draped an arm over the back of the couch behind me. "We're here to enjoy the fact we're all still alive. Nothing more."

"That is something to celebrate." My mind kept

returning to Mary. She filled my dreams. Her and Brutus. Him trying to force himself on a dying woman… I woke with the urge to throw up. And to punch my sister and Zachary for having any part in that. They'd clearly taken women who looked like me in the hope of making it harder to find me. Hunting down one brown eyed brunette amongst several would have been difficult. Mary was dead because she looked like me. Not for any other reason.

"Here we go," Hunter muttered.

Chloe blinked hard and shook her head. Her head flopped to one side, then the other. Her eyes rolled back and she slumped onto the couch.

"She's—" I started to stand, but Slade pressed a hand to my shoulder, keeping me down.

"Not dead," he said. "She's not fully unconscious either. Just…incapacitated."

My eyes widened as a couple of fellow students, second years like the twins, approached Chloe, smiles on their faces.

Her eyes were still open. They widened. Fear. Understanding. Terror.

A chill passed right through me.

"They're not going to…"

"It's what she arranged for you to go through," Hunter said, his tone dark with simmering rage. Every drop directed at Chloe.

"She organised for you to be sold to someone who would force themselves on you. She wanted you broken. We're returning the favour." He smiled and gulped the last of his beer.

The two guys hooked their shoulders under Chloe's arms and pulled her to her feet. One held her upright before the other scooped her into his arms.

I must have imagined hearing her whimper, because the music in the bar was too loud for that. She was virtually paralysed. Completely unable to fight back against what they'd do to her. It wouldn't just be the two of them either. They would use her and use her until—

I shot up out of my seat so fast I spilled vodka all over my hand. I barely noticed.

"We can't let them do that to her. I know what she would have done to me, but... I just can't. Please. Make it stop."

"Of course—" Before Hunter could finish his sentence, Dane stalked into the room.

He saw the two guys with Chloe and his face turned red.

"What the fuck are you doing?" he demanded.

The one carrying her smiled as though they weren't up to anything. "Hi, sir. She fell asleep. We were going to take her to her room and tuck her in."

Dane gave them both a disbelieving look and all

but hauled Chloe into his own arms. "I'll take her from here."

"I'm sure you will, sir," the other student said. He grinned and ducked away before Dane could respond.

Dane glanced over at me and my guys. His eyes narrowed, but he must have caught sight of the worry in my eyes. The sides of his mouth drew back, but he nodded and carried Chloe out of the bar.

"Mission accomplished." Hunter looked smug.

I sat back down, feeling numb. "You weren't planning to let them rape her?"

He shrugged. "If that happened, it happened. But this way, Chloe and Dane no longer trust Zachary. He bought her a drink and then left. Does that say suspicious as fuck to you?"

"Who was really on the phone?" I asked.

"His grandmother," Slade said. "Nice lady. Very receptive to a healthy deposit into her bank account." He looked as smug as Hunter.

I closed my eyes for a moment. "You bribed Zachary's grandmother to call him up and pretend there's some emergency?" After a moment I added, "Or was there a real emergency?"

"Oh, it's real." Parker grinned. "But I'm sure he'll be able to help get her kitten out of that tree."

If anyone would consider that to be an emergency, it would be my former step grandmother. She was very attached to her cats.

"She'll let us know when he leaves her place to come back here," Slade added.

"Trust you to sweet talk an old lady," I told him.

He grinned. "Like I said, she's a nice woman. I'm definitely going to try the cake recipe she emailed me."

"You sweet talk old ladies and you cook." I shook my head in amazement. "Who even are you?"

He laughed. "One of the guys who would do anything for you." He leaned in and kissed my mouth.

"You know if Zachary manages to get back in with Chloe, they're going to retaliate for this," I said. "If Dane hadn't arrived when he did…"

"You would have stopped it." Slade took my hand and squeezed lightly. "Chloe would have been grateful."

"Was that part of the plan too?" I asked.

The guys all exchanged a glance.

"That was a variable we couldn't one hundred percent factor in," Parker said. "There was every chance Tyson and Felix could have had her right here in front of everyone and you would have sat back and watched. Personally, I couldn't see you doing that. Not even after what she did to you."

"Don't mistake me for a good person," I warned. "I just... I couldn't see any woman go through what Danica did. What Mary almost did. Chloe might have been happy to have it happened to me, but that doesn't mean I have to do the same to her."

I exhaled softly. "Maybe my dad is right, I'm not cut out to lead the family. I'm not ruthless enough."

"You definitely are," Slade said. "There's a fine line between being ruthless and being an asshole. Hunter, Parker and I walk that line, so you don't have to."

"You all would have let it happen to her?" I looked from one to the other, to the other.

"I would have brought the popcorn." Parker grinned.

"I would have brought the beer," Hunter said.

"I would have helped them eat and drink it," Slade said. "It might have been the thing that forced her to step aside and stop competing with you. It might have prevented whatever she might do after this. There may come a day when you wish it happened."

I chewed over that thought for a moment. Long enough to realise he was right. If I was going to win this thing, I was going to have to toughen the fuck up. Whatever that took.

I should have been horrified that the guys would let my twin sister be raped, but it cemented the fact there was nothing they wouldn't do for me. No length they wouldn't go to.

"It makes you feel any better, I wouldn't have touched her," Hunter said.

"Me either," Parker agreed.

"Me three." Slade nodded firmly. "Not unless that was something you needed me to do." I couldn't tell what he thought of that idea.

There was no way that should have been hot, but it fucking was. For half a second I enjoyed the thought of Slade holding Chloe down and ramming himself into her. Her cries of pain and anguish…

Yeah, I was as fucked up as they were.

CHAPTER 15

LILA

I didn't see Zachary before he grabbed me from behind, whirled me around and pressed me against the corridor wall, his body against mine. His hand closed around my throat.

"Fucking psycho bitch," he growled. "Don't think I don't know what you did to Chloe." His breath was hot on my cheek.

"I didn't do anything to Chloe," I said as evenly as I could with my heart racing. I hated the fact he took me by surprise, but I composed myself. My father would be proud of me for recovering so quickly.

"Never show them fear, or they know they have you by the balls," he would have said.

I tipped my chin up and stared Zachary down, unflinching. "You're the one who seems to enjoy spiking people's drinks."

His hand tightened. "I didn't do anything to her. I sure as fuck didn't *drug* her."

"Says you," I retorted. "What's wrong? Chloe and Dane don't believe you're not involved?" Judging by the flicker of anger on his face, that was exactly the case. Exactly what the twins and Slade wanted.

"Don't tell me, Chloe won't suck your dick anymore?" I gave him a smile laced with sarcasm.

He glared at me. "Maybe I should make you suck my dick instead."

"Only if you want me to bite it off." There was no way my mouth was going anywhere near his cock.

He pressed me harder into the wall, then stepped back and crossed his arms.

"It's a shame Chloe's plan didn't work. I would have paid money to watch whoever bought you break you. Hell, I would have settled for photos of the mascara running down your face."

"And you call me a fucking psycho," I retorted. "What sort of sick fuck arranges for women to be abducted and sold?"

"Your father," he suggested. "Have you ever done anything to stop him? Have you ever said a single fucking word? Or have you let it go on for years and years? How many women have been raped while you did nothing?"

I managed to contain a flinch. "I didn't know any

better. Now I do. It won't be happening when I take over the family. I sure as hell wouldn't organise for someone to be taken just to get them out of the way."

"No, you'd organise for your sister to be drugged and raped by her classmates for your own amusement. Let me guess, Hunter, Parker and Slade were going to take their turns with her too. You're all as fucked up in the head as each other."

"Hypocrisy isn't a good look for you," I told him. "I did nothing to Chloe. If Dane hadn't stepped in when he did, I would have."

Zachary gave a bitter laugh. "Bullshit. You wouldn't have done a single thing."

"What would you have done?" I asked. "Like I said, you're the one who likes to spike drinks. Did you drug hers just to see if you could have some fun with her? Maybe you like fucking women when they're unconscious."

He dropped his hands, lunged towards me and pinned me to the wall again. "Maybe I should find out." He pressed his growing erection into the side of my hip.

"Maybe I should cut off your balls and have them made into dumplings for Chloe to eat." I managed to keep my voice even. "Oh, right. They'd only be a tiny mouthful. Barely more than a few crumbs."

"You think so?" He ground his now hard cock against me. "It seems like you need a reminder."

I looked him straight in the eyes. "We both know you're not going to cheat on Chloe, even if it means not getting to work your anger out on me." If he tried, he'd find himself in a thousand tiny pieces, courtesy of me and my guys.

He ground against me a moment longer before grunting and stepping back. "I wouldn't soil my cock on your tainted pussy."

I managed a short breath of relief.

"That might be the most romantic thing a guy has ever said to me," I said sarcastically. "My pussy is way too good for your cock."

He stalked over to a window that overlooked a courtyard. "This is all bullshit." He ran a hand over his hair. "You have no idea what you've done. Chloe and Dane both think I did that to her. Nothing I say… I wouldn't do that. I love her."

Cry me a motherfucking river.

"Is this where you expect me to go to her and tell her you weren't involved?" I asked. "That you didn't really try to blow her up?"

He turned around, looking stricken. "I did not try to blow her up. That was—"

"Meant for me," I finished for him. "Placed there

by her to convince me to trust her. For what? To give her more time to put her plan together? Didn't have enough brunettes who looked like me?"

He averted his eyes.

"I thought so. I'm not saying I was involved in what happened to her, but the only way I'd tell her you weren't is if you convinced her to pull out of this competition with me."

If she did that, I wouldn't give a shit what she did and who she did it with. Let her, Dane and Zachary run off into the sunset together. If I never saw them again, that would be all right with me.

"She would never listen to me. Not while she thinks I drugged her." He looked delightfully miserable.

I shrugged. "Well, then, it seems we have nothing more to say to each other." I started to turn away.

"What if I told you what she had planned?" He looked desperate. "You can stop it from happening and then speak to her for me."

Now he had me thinking. If I knew what to look for, I could avoid it. I could stop my guys from getting hurt, or worse. Maybe I could turn whatever it was, back on her. She could be the one abducted and sold next time.

"What makes you think I'd believe a word you

say?" I asked carefully. "This could all be an act to set me up."

"It could be, but it isn't." His eyes pleaded with me to believe him. "I don't give a shit about this competition between you and Chloe anymore. All I want is her." His thick brows lowered.

"Do you think she'll want you if you do anything that makes her lose?" I asked.

"I'll convince her she doesn't need to win this. There are more important things in life than power."

"If the idea of touching you wasn't repulsive, I'd check to see if you have a high temperature," I said. "Since when did Zachary Sinclair not care about power?"

It was what all of us were raised to want. To please my father and to gain as much power as possible. Personal fulfilment didn't factor into it.

"When I saw Chloe looking at me with mistrust." His brow crinkled as he frowned. "She asked me to organise for your drink and the twin's drinks to be spiked. She didn't know who it was behind the bar that did it. She didn't want to know. I swore to her the guy I hired left. Whoever you hired—"

"I didn't hire anyone," I said coldly.

He shook his head. "Whoever the fuck the twins hired then. Or Slade. Whatever. It wasn't me."

"Studying at Brutham Academy will teach you a

lot of things." I folded my arms over my breasts. "Including the fact you should never trust anyone to pour a drink. Not unless you know they won't drug you. Your asshole quit and ran and you didn't think he might be replaced?"

He shrugged. "I should have anticipated. I didn't. I'm paying the price for that."

Boo fucking hoo, I thought.

"I'm going to be honest with you, Zachary," I said. "I don't think you've even begun to pay the price for what you, my sister and Dane did to me. Starting with the toxic gas and ending with the whole trafficking bullshit. Now I think about it, you've all gotten off lightly. I don't want to know what Chloe has planned for me, because we'll be ready for her. We will go after her again and there's nothing she can do to get ready for what we'll do. When we're done, she'll beg to step down."

He glared at me. "You're going to regret that. When Chloe is done with you, you'll be the one begging to step down." He stepped closer. "You'll be begging to be auctioned off to someone who will only use you. Because what's coming is going to be so much worse than that."

I wanted to slap the smug expression off his face. Instead, I rolled my eyes at his melodramatic statement. He should be studying theatre instead of chemistry.

"You have no idea what she's planning, do you? It absolutely kills you that you haven't got a clue and that whatever she does, you won't be involved. You might as well leave Brutham and go back to ANU. Make a life for yourself away from us and all this." I spread my hands to either side.

"You never know, you might even be happy." I would be. The farther away from me he was, the better.

He rubbed the back of his neck and exhaled in frustration. "I'm not going anywhere, Lila. If you won't help me voluntarily, then I might have to find a way to force you to."

"Have you ever considered asking nicely?" I asked. "Instead, you accosted me, threatened to assault me, then threatened me in three or four other ways too. I know for a fact your mother raised you better than that." Not much better, granted. She wouldn't have married my father otherwise.

"Yes, but your father didn't." He smiled viciously. "Your father taught us to be ruthless and merciless, and fight for what we want. Not to roll over and play dead."

"Then go out there and fight for Chloe." I waved down the corridor. "Don't let her tell you no. She might like it if you pinned her to the wall and made her listen."

He looked at me for a few drawn out movements.

"You're wrong about one thing. I do know what she's planning. She had a backup in case things went pear-shaped with the last plan. She probably has a backup for the backup. I believe you when you say you didn't drug her. It's something the twins would do. Something half-assed and ultimately doomed to fail. I mean, what have they really done? Changed her birth-control and put her to sleep for a while? Small potatoes compared to what we've done. What will they think of next? Putting hair dye in her shampoo so she accidentally dyes her hair green? They make all of this look like amateur hour in preschool. They call themselves evil twins, but pathetic twins would be more accurate. It's almost like they want you to lose."

He looked down his nose at me, then stepped away.

I pressed my head back against the wall behind me. He was right. We hadn't done anything that came close to what Chloe had done to us. I knew the guys fully intended drugging Chloe to go a lot further than it did. Were they disappointed I stopped it? Was I wrong to think about stepping in? This whole competition could be over if I'd kept my mouth shut and if Dane hadn't stepped in when he did.

I was going to have to do something drastic. Something that would have an impact on Chloe and on this stupid competition. Something that would put an end to it once and for all.

CHAPTER 16

LILA

"We have something for you." Hunter waved Parker and Slade into my room and closed and locked the door behind them. He held up a tub of my favourite choc-mint ice cream. In his other hand, he held a bottle of chocolate sauce.

They sat down around me on my bed. Parker handed out bowls and spoons and Hunter started scooping ice cream into each.

"Are we celebrating something?" I put my laptop aside and nodded as Slade raised the bottle of chocolate sauce and looked at me in question. He squeezed a big dollop onto the top of my ice cream.

"We're celebrating being alive," Hunter said. "In my opinion, that's a good enough excuse for ice cream." He raised his bowl to me in toast before starting to eat.

"Works for me." I dug my spoon into mine. "You're sure there's nothing in this other than ice cream and chocolate sauce, right?"

"Slade and I drove into town to get it," Hunter said. "If there's anything in there, then someone was trying to drug the whole town."

"You realise that's not impossible, right?" I still scooped ice cream into my mouth and savoured the minty taste before I swallowed. "Mmm, so good."

Parker grinned around his spoon. "You have the exact same expression on your face right now as you do when you swallow my cum."

"What can I say? I have good taste in ice cream and men." And ice cream and cum both tasted delicious.

"I wonder how much of this I'd have to eat before my cum tasted like mint," Parker mused.

"There's only one way to find out," Hunter said.

"Are you offering to take part in that experiment?" Slade teased.

Hunter laughed. "Only on the coming side, not the swallowing. In order for this to be a true scientific experiment, we need a control group. Or a control guy."

"As interested as I am in scientific research and Lila swallowing my cum, I don't want to miss out on this ice cream." Slade shovelled a huge spoonful into his mouth.

"That experiment will have to wait for another day then," Hunter said. "I wonder if the Academy will give us a grant for the research."

"I don't think so, because it would be difficult to prove or replicate the results," I said. "But that doesn't mean we can't conduct the experiment anyway." I finished my ice cream and set the bowl aside on the table beside the bed.

"I propose a different experiment." Parker placed his bowl on top of mine and grabbed up the chocolate sauce. "It's called, let's see how delicious chocolate sauce is when licked off Lila's skin."

He pressed me down to the mattress and pushed my singlet up, over my bare breasts. He turned the bottle upside down and trickled sauce over my breasts and stomach.

"She certainly *looks* delicious." Hunter spooned himself some more ice cream and sat with his legs crossed, watching.

Slade put his own bowl aside, grabbed a handful of my singlet and pulled it up over my arms and head. "Wouldn't want to get sauce on that. Or this." He scooted down and pulled my shorts and panties down my legs and off my feet.

"She looks even more delicious like that," Hunter remarked.

"My theory is that the taste of her skin will make the chocolate sauce even better. My method will be to use my tongue to lick it off. I'll measure the results using a very scientific method; my taste buds." Parker grinned at me, then lay with his head over me before starting to oh-so-slowly tease me with the tip of his tongue.

He swirled his tongue around my nipple, stopping every few moments to swallow the sauce.

Slade parted my legs with his hands and lowered his face to my pussy.

"What, no scientific hypothesis?" Hunter asked with mock outrage.

Slade looked back up and grinned. "My theory is that if I lick Lila's clit, not only will she taste like perfection, I'll give her the best orgasm of her entire life. Best to date. There's always room for improvement."

Hunter nodded, evidently satisfied. "The first part of your theory is sound. The second part is presumptuous and, in my not-particularly-humble opinion, bullshit. While I can't scientifically prove the fact, I'm almost certain I have given her the best orgasms of her life. To date. However, I completely support this scientific research, if it means our queen gets an orgasm. Or two. Continue. The results of the second part of your theory will have to be measured by Lila herself. Parker and I will take note of how loud she screams. That will be factored into the results."

"Thank you Doctor Brantley," Slade said with a grin.

"You're welcome, Mr Lincoln." Hunter wiggled his eyebrows, then went on eating.

I shook my head at them all. They were too fucking adorable for their own good. I lay back and let my gaze drift to the ceiling while Slade lowered his mouth to me and resumed the experiment. I much preferred science to business, and this was definitely the kind of experiment I could get behind.

The combination of both of their tongues on my most sensitive places, had me trembling in moments. My whole body ignited slowly. My blood burned its way through my system, pulsing through my pussy and making me ache. The things these guys did to me was nothing short of absolute bliss.

"Chocolate sauce never tasted so good," Parker moaned. He had a mouthful of that and one of my nipples. "I'm spoiled now."

"To be fair, you were spoiled a long time ago," Hunter teased.

I glanced down as Parker flipped Hunter off. I watched Slade's head bobbing up and down as he licked me from top to bottom. He slid a finger inside me, working it in and around in circles.

I quivered and groaned from the sensation.

He locked his eyes on mine as he added another finger to the first.

"I don't remember fingers being part of the experiment," Hunter remarked. "However, since our subject matter is clearly enjoying herself, I'm happy to endorse this modification."

Parker raised his head from my nipple long enough to say, "You're such a nerd."

Hunter chuckled. "Only when it comes to pleasing our girl. There are no lengths I won't go to in the pursuit of that goal."

I snort-laughed and watched Parker sucking my tit while I drew closer and closer to the precipice. Even with everything crazy going on, I was still the luckiest woman in the country, if not the world.

Right from the start, the twins made it their mission to treat me like a queen. Slade had apparently accepted that mission too. I loved every minute of it. Every woman deserves to be treated like she's special. Like she's the centre of her partners' universe. The sun their existence revolves around. They made me feel like all of that and more.

"I'm so close," I whispered.

"Don't let her come yet," Hunter said. "I want this

to be amazing for her. When she does come, I want her to scream the place down."

Slade slid his fingers out of me and traced circles around the insides of my thigh. He kissed his way down and back up the other one.

At the same time, Parker sucked and nipped my nipples and breasts, not letting up for a moment.

I made a small sound of annoyance in the back of my throat, frustrated at being denied an orgasm so close to the edge. Hunter was right, I would scream the place down, but it still drove me crazy, and he knew it.

After what felt like a year, Slade finally returned his mouth to the centre of my pussy. He drew my clit between his lips, then bit down lightly.

I moaned. "Mmm, that feels amazing."

"You taste amazing," Parker told me. He moved up enough to kiss me, his mouth tasting of chocolate with a hint of salt and mint. If we could bottle that, we'd make a fortune.

I licked his lips and plunged my tongue into his mouth. I couldn't get enough of him. Of any of them. They were as much a part of me and my world as breathing, or my heart beating.

Slade slid his fingers back inside, three of them now. He fucked me with his hand and tongue, driving me hard to bliss and over the edge.

I came, groaning into Parker's mouth. He swallowed my scream and gave it back with a moan of his own.

I rocked my hips against Slade's fingers and mouth, drawing out the pleasure, letting the light dance across my vision. Blood roared through me like a cascade of water rushing over a waterfall. It went on and on until I finally, slowly drifted back to earth. I flopped back against the mattress and panted through my nose, my lips never leaving Parker's.

"I think we can call that experiment more or less successful," Hunter said.

"It was very successful," Slade said. "I can confirm Lila tastes delicious." He grinned.

"I can confirm that finding to be accurate," Parker agreed, his mouth pressed against mine. "With or without chocolate sauce."

"You know what else tastes good with chocolate sauce?" Hunter asked. He arched an eyebrow at me.

"Beer?" I asked teasingly, knowing exactly what he was referring to. I laughed at the horrified expressions on all of their faces. "Right, you meant pizza."

"Getting warmer." Hunter undid his jeans and curled his fingers under his cock to pull it free.

"Sausage pizza?" I watched with interest as he worked his cock, making it hard.

"How about just sausage?" He moved over to me and handed me the bottle of chocolate sauce.

I took it and trickled a line of sauce from his head, halfway down his cock. I handed the bottle to Parker and leaned down to run my tongue across the trail.

"Sausage and chocolate, perfect combination." He tasted sweet and salty, hot from his blood and cool from the sauce. I licked pre-cum from his tip before sliding my mouth all the way onto his cock. I sucked him and the divine chocolate flavour. I always liked sucking cock, but this was next level.

He moved his hips, driving himself in and out of my mouth. He tangled his fingers in my hair and held me there as he fucked my mouth.

"So fucking perfect," he breathed. "Such a good, amazing queen. You have the best, fucking mouth." He thrust a few more times. "I'm going to come in your mouth. Right down your pretty little throat. But don't swallow. You're going to hold my cum."

He twitched, grinding into me before he came, squirting salty, hot cum out his slit.

"So fucking perfect," he breathed. "But we're going to try another experiment. Parker." He waved for his twin to take his place.

"We're going to see how much cum Lila can hold in her mouth before she has to swallow."

I raised my eyebrows at him, but this was a challenge I was happy to accept. I held his cum in the side of my mouth as Parker slid his cock inside.

Every few thrusts, he'd pull all the way out to let me breathe through my nose.

"You feel so good," Parker groaned. With every stroke, the tip of his cock dipped into his twin's cum, until he was soaked with that and my saliva, along with his own juices.

He grunted and pounded harder a couple of times before he squirted his own cum into my mouth.

"Can you hold it for a while longer?" Hunter asked.

I nodded. I focused on breathing through my nose and combining both releases into one. When I was ready, I opened my mouth again for Slade's cock.

"Holy shit," Slade said breathlessly. "I feel like it should be weird to stick my cock into two other guys' cum, but this is…"

I glanced up to see him shake his head. I had no words for it either. This was one of the hottest things I'd ever done.

I closed my eyes and concentrated on breathing, sucking and keeping myself from swallowing too hard. Fighting the reflex wasn't easy, but I wanted to wait until I had all three of them inside me. I wanted to combine all of them in one big, delicious mouthful.

Fortunately, Slade only took a few more thrusts before he came, adding his cum to the wet, salty ball of heat.

I drew my mouth back off him, took a couple of breaths through my nose, then slowly and deliberately swallowed down every single drop.

"Woman, you are a fucking goddess," Hunter said.

"And a goddess of fucking," Parker agreed.

"Hell yeah I am." I smiled. "I think that just qualified me for some sort of degree in science."

"I don't know," Hunter said slowly. "I think we need more experiments before we get to that level."

"A lot more," Slade said. "By the time you all graduate, you'll do it with honours."

"Yeah, we will."

We had to survive that long first.

CHAPTER 17

PARKER

"This is so unfair," I stated.

"What is?" Lila sat on the step below me, between my legs. I played with her ponytail, twisting the soft strands around my fingers before letting them fall free.

"That we don't get to sit in on the board meeting," I said. "I'd like to be a fly on the wall in there."

"This will have to do." Hunter tapped the laptop that rested on his knees. "We'll see most of it through the feed."

"Unless they figured out we hacked it last time to watch," I pointed out.

"How would they know?" Hunter shrugged. "Most people here wouldn't bother."

"Most people here don't have the last name Bell or

Brantley," Slade said. "We have a vested interest in knowing what the school board is discussing."

"Couldn't you wrangle an invitation?" I asked. "You do work here."

"Only the board and the department heads are invited," Slade said. "Not humble guys like me."

"I don't know if humble is a word I'd use to describe you," I told him.

He smiled briefly. "Probably not. I also have to pretend I don't know you're doing this. If the board found out, I'd be fired."

"Fired if you're lucky," Hunter said. "Shallow grave if you're not. The school board takes their meetings seriously."

"That's my father's car." Lila nodded towards the window beside the stairs. The window was covered with vines, giving us a limited view out, but making it difficult for anyone to see in.

"Looks like Reuben is right behind him," I said. "You'd think they'd share a car."

Hunter snickered. "I don't know who would kill whom first if they got in a car together."

"It wouldn't be pretty," Lila said. She craned her neck. "Yeah, that's Reuben. Mac D'Antonio is with him. And Hilton Blake."

"If they're not careful, the school will sink under the weight of all those billionaires," I joked.

I watched my brother and his—friends wasn't quite the word—until they disappeared into the building. Somehow, the air in the place got heavier, like a shadow passed over the Academy. That wasn't far wrong. The combined evil deeds of the school board would make the average person shudder. If their power didn't make them horny as hell.

"Here we go." Hunter tapped the keyboard and brought up the feed. The camera off to the side of the board room showed a table surrounded by thick, leather chairs. Several men and a couple of women already reclined in them. All of the men were members of the Brotherhood of Kings. The women were, no doubt, aware of its existence. Neither looked deterred. Of course not. If they had enough power to sit on the school board of Brutham Academy, they wouldn't be intimidated by anyone here.

Hunter already decided Lila would sit on the board someday. Him too if he could swing it. I'd be happy to watch from home. Or hear about it all later.

The sound of shuffling and low conversation came through the laptop speakers. No one seemed in a hurry to take their chair.

"Please be seated." The Academy's principal stepped around to the end of the table and stood with his palms pressed against the mahogany timber.

The shuffling persisted for another few minutes before silence fell.

"Thank you all for coming." The principal droned on with his standard welcome, along with a reminder of the minutes of the last meeting and notes about things which needed to be discussed at this one.

Most of it was boring as shit. School funding, the discussion to expand or contract certain departments, or combine others. The board could argue for hours over all of that and not come to any conclusions. No one ever wanted their department to be cut back. No one wanted their children or sibling's degrees to be compromised.

Reuben sat on the opposite side of the table from Samuel Bell. Every so often, one would look at the other like they expected trouble. That was nothing out of the ordinary either. This was the only time they tolerated being in the same room as each other.

Sometimes, I wondered if our hope for the two families to come together was in vain. Old hate and animosity seemed hard to put aside.

"Are these meetings always so boring?" Lila asked.

"Usually, unless someone gets shot," Hunter said. "That's when things get really interesting. Mostly we watch because sometimes they change things up with the trials. We don't want to be taken by surprise."

"Yeah, there was the time—" I started to say.

Hunter hissed at me to be quiet.

"I assume you received the request to consider the founding of a Brutham Academy campus in Dusk Bay?" Reuben asked.

"We did," the principal replied carefully. "That's on the agenda to discuss today."

"Let's discuss it now," Reuben said. "The funding is there. Adequate land was donated. I see no reason to delay."

"That's Reuben," I muttered. "Straight to the point." He'd be more interested in his own personal agenda than the rest of the board's priorities.

"Why does he want a campus there so badly?" Slade frowned.

"If I had to guess, I'd say Caleb is pissed about us disrupting his operation. He's probably the one pushing for this. If he could arrange it, he'd sidestep Reuben and Reuben wouldn't want that. In proposing it himself, he puts himself in charge. Caleb gets what he wants, but on Reuben's terms." Hunter waved at us again to be quiet.

"We don't want to be hasty," the principal said. "There is much to be discussed—"

"I suggest we put it to a vote," Reuben said. "We

can work on the logistics later. Let's come to an agreement first."

"Your father looks like you when he's suspicious as fuck," I told Lila, speaking softly in her ear. "I can almost see him thinking. Wondering what Reuben is planning."

"I'm wondering that myself," she whispered. "Why would anyone want another Brutham campus?"

"More people to play Kink or Drink?" I grinned.

She choked back a snort. "I can't imagine Caleb taking part in anything like that."

I chuckled. "Probably not. Chances are, he and those he works with would like somewhere closer to home for their children and prospective children. I'm surprised it's taken them this long."

The principal looked uncomfortable, but nodded. "Very well. All in favour of a Dusk Bay campus, raise your hand."

Not surprisingly, Reuben, Mac and Hilton raised their hands. So did a few others. Samuel kept his hand firmly down at the table.

"One, two, three, four, five, six... Seven," Hunter counted. "That's more than half of the thirteen board members. Looks like the Academy is expanding."

"Reuben looks smug as fuck," I remarked.

"When does Reuben *not* looked smug as fuck?" Hunter asked.

I pointed a finger gun at him. "Good point. But he looks particularly smug right now."

"Well isn't this cosy?" Chloe drawled from behind us. "You know you're not supposed to be spying on the school board meetings, right?

"There's a lot of stuff we're technically not supposed to do, but do you see that stopping any of us?" I asked without looking back.

"It certainly doesn't stop you," she agreed. She walked down until she was standing beside Lila. "I'm sure you're pleased to see me alive and well."

"I don't think pleased is the word that comes to mind," Lila told her dryly. "Anyway, shouldn't you be having this conversation with Zachary? He was the one who drugged all of us at one time or another. That sounds like the behaviour of a psychopath to me. Thank fuck you found out now and not when you were in deeper."

"Zachary was in pretty deep from what Hunter and I heard," I remarked. "Balls deep."

Chloe gave me a dirty look. "We'll deal with Zachary when the time is right. He...misjudged."

I wanted to laugh in her face for really believing Zachary went after her. It's true what they say. It's hard to gain trust, but as easy as fuck to lose it. I had no doubt Zachary was working on some way to worm himself back in with her. If not, that was his problem. Personally, I didn't give a shit.

Lila did laugh. "Misjudged? He set you up. I'd call that a whole lot more than a misjudgement. What sort of person does that to a woman? Ah, right. Someone like you. You're lucky you didn't wake up in the back of a truck."

Chloe shrugged. "You don't seem the worse for the experience. You know what they say, what doesn't kill you makes you stronger."

"It makes you a whole lot more than stronger," Lila said. "It also makes you pissed off and vengeful. What you did was…disgusting. Cruel."

"You wish you'd thought of it?" Chloe asked with mock sweetness.

"I do," I said before Lila could respond. "But if we had, we would have been more successful. No one would have seen you ever again. Except whoever bought you." I looked her up and down deliberately, as though appraising her value.

"You're sick," she told me.

I grinned. "It takes one to know one. You were the one who came up with it. And the one who wanted to use Hunter and I as… What was it? Leverage. Did you really think Reuben was going to give you anything in return for us?"

"Who said anything about Reuben?" she replied easily. "He has plenty of enemies who would love to get their hands on you. *You* have plenty of enemies who'd like to get their hands on you, too. It's a very long list."

"You know what they say about needing to break eggs to make omelettes," I replied. "We do what we have to do, the same way anyone else in this world does. No one can blame us for that. And if they can, too fucking bad. At the end of the day, we're the ones still standing. Us and Lila. We'll be the ones standing at the end too."

I was tempted to push her down the stairs and be done with it, but I suspected the fall wouldn't be enough to end her. She'd break a bone or two at worst. Then go crying to daddy, no doubt. Pity.

"Keep telling yourself that," she replied. "That doesn't make it true. Honestly, I'm surprised you haven't given up yet. You can still do that. Make it easier on yourselves and walk away now. It will be a lot easier for you if you do." She gave Lila a filthy look before heading away, down the stairs.

"I can't believe we just accused Reuben of being smug," I remarked. "If anyone is smug, it's her."

Not for much longer.

CHAPTER 18

PARKER

"She's got balls, showing up here," Hunter muttered.

He drank a gulp of beer and toasted Chloe and Dane as they made their way through the bar and sat on one of the couches. "How nice of you to join us. Kink or Drink wouldn't be the same without you."

"Of course it wouldn't," Chloe said. She wore a pale pink T-shirt that matched her nail polish, and a short black skirt that fell to mid thigh. The side of her short hair was held back by a bright pink hair clip.

I didn't know who she was trying to fool with the innocent exterior, but it wasn't fooling any of us. We knew how acidic her heart really was.

"Someone has to keep an eye on you." Dane draped an arm over the back of the couch behind Chloe. He gave us all a dark look.

"That's very noble of you," Hunter said sarcastically, but without his smile faltering.

"We have some new faces. And some old faces." Annoyance flickered in his eyes when Zachary entered the bar and strode over towards us. He sat down between a couple of women and crossed his legs.

My gaze slid over to Chloe. Neither she nor Dane seemed surprised to see Zachary, but they didn't seem happy about it either. Apparently they hadn't kissed and made up yet.

I exchanged a glance with Hunter. His smirk suggested he was thinking the same thing. I laced my fingers in Lila's and squeezed.

I leaned to whisper in her ear. "Any time you want to leave, just say the word."

She responded with a subtle nod of her head. "I won't let them ruin all of my fun. I came here tonight to show them I'm not broken, not even close. I want to do something normal."

I wasn't sure if our little card game was normal but I knew what she meant. She was a university student. That meant lots of study, but also lots of… Drinking and fucking. She didn't want to let the rivalry between her and her sister stop her from enjoying herself.

"Ah, here's Slade." Hunter rubbed his hands together and grinned.

Slade balanced a tray of empty shot glasses on the palm of one hand and held two bottles of tequila in the other.

"We figured with the unfortunate spate of drug-gings, we'd forgo pre-poured drinks." Hunter nodded his thanks to Slade as he placed the tray and the bottles on the table. "Anyone is welcome to inspect the bottles to make sure they haven't been tampered with." He looked around the gathered students, but no one moved.

"Very well then." Hunter picked up his pack of Kink or Drink cards from the table and started to shuffle them. "There have been suggestions in the past that I may have put the cards in a particular order. I might have been slightly remiss in not shuffling them. From now on, they will be carefully shuffled. If anyone wants a turn, you're welcome to do that too."

He split the deck before flicking the corners of the cards to combine the deck in a different order.

"I think we can see they are shuffled." Slade sat on the other side of Lila.

"Thank you," Hunter said graciously. "I wouldn't want to be accused of cheating."

Dane barked a laugh. "If the hat fits."

"I don't have as much life experience as you do," Hunter said slowly, "but I've noticed that people who tend to fling accusations are trying to deflect from their own shortcomings or guilt."

Dane looked ready to pick up one of the tequila bottles and smash Hunter over the head with it. Chloe placed a hand on his knee, keeping him from doing anything rash.

In the corner of my eye, I saw Zachary watching both of them like a stalker. He wasn't even trying to contain his envy. He wanted to be the one with Chloe's hand on his knee. No doubt he'd also be having the same thoughts about smashing a bottle over Hunter's head.

If I'm honest, I've had thoughts like that myself from time to time. Being a twin wasn't always torture and fucking around with people. Sometimes it was difficult, especially when we spent so much time together.

"Are we going to play?" one of the newer students asked. What was her name? Tina? She sat with a couple of women I'd seen her with before. All second years like me, most of them were studying business and marketing. Even businesses like ours needed good PR from time to time.

"Of course we are." Hunter placed the pack of

cards face down on the table. "Would you care to go first?" He gestured towards Tina.

She looked uncertain now, but her friends giggled and waved for her to go ahead.

"You've got this." Angie was a perky blonde with perky breasts. Breasts I would happily have touched, if not for Lila. And by touched, I mean come all over.

Tina leaned forward, giving us all an eyeful of cleavage, and picked up a card. Her eyes grew round, but she looked excited.

"Get choked," she read. "I've always wanted to, but all the guys seem to think they'll hurt me." She pouted.

All the guys were silly if that's what they thought. It was just a matter of learning the right pressure by paying attention to your partner.

She looked around hopefully.

"I'll do it," Zachary said before any of the other guys could speak. Tina's friends moved aside to make room for him to sit beside her. He stroked his palm down the side of her face, over her chin and down to her throat. She tilted her head back as he gripped her with his large hand.

"Does that feel good?" He braced himself with his other hand on the back of the couch beside her.

"So good," she said breathlessly. "I'm so wet now."

Her eyes were half closed. She looked like she'd come with a breath on her clit.

"Of course you are," he said, his voice deep. A moment before I thought he might take it too hard and strangle her, he slipped his hand away and moved to the other side of the couch. His eyes were dark. He'd come close to giving in to the temptation to kill her.

Lucky for him because he wouldn't be allowed to play this game again.

Lucky for her too, because being choked was supposed to be fun.

I glanced over at Chloe. She was visibly fuming. Of course, that was the exact reaction Zachary wanted from her. To piss her off, make her jealous.

She glared at him, then looked away. Apparently forgiving and forgetting didn't come easily to her.

Fair enough. It didn't come easily to me either. I was good at a lot of things, including holding a grudge.

Zachary grunted something, then stood and stalked out of the bar.

"He looks like someone who needs to get laid more often," Hunter remarked. "Parker, do you want the next turn?"

I shrugged. "Sure." Anything to break the tension.

I leaned over and snagged the card at the top of

the pile. I held it in front of me for a few moments for dramatic effect before turning it around to read it.

I blinked a couple of times. My face heated.

"Bro, are you blushing?" Hunter asked. "What does the card say?"

I cleared my throat and swallowed. "Get pegged."

"May I remind you that taking a drink is an option?" Hunter asked.

"Yeah, I…" I rubbed a hand over the back of my neck. "I'll try anything once."

I looked sideways at Lila. She was watching me with dark, curious eyes. With no judgement at all.

"You want to?" I asked. "There's a strap on over there." I jerked my head towards the shelves of toys. Everything was cleaned and sterilised between uses, which meant they were constantly being cleaned and sterilised. Brutham Academy students tended to be adventurous. Probably because none of us expected to live long, so we might as well make the best of it.

"Only if you want to," she said.

I placed the card face up on the table and offered her my hand. She curled her fingers around mine and we made our way over to the side of the room.

"Any time you're uncomfortable…" She gave me a gentle smile.

"I know." I nodded. "The safe word here is banana." I wasn't used to the nervous excitement that passed through me. Excitement yes, but not nerves. This was something I had no experience with. The second later, I realised it was likely she didn't either. That helped to settle my nerves somewhat.

"Okay, let's see if we can figure out how this goes on." I grabbed the strap on and held it in front of Lila. She slipped out of her skirt and panties, totally unfazed at being half naked in front of everyone else. She never had been shy about stripping and fucking in public. Fortunately, neither had I.

She gripped the sides and held it in place while I walked around her to fasten and tighten it. Satisfied it wasn't going to fall down, I stepped back around to face her.

I grinned. "That's a good look for you." The straps were black, but the dildo that stuck out from the front was bright pink. It wasn't massive either, thank fuck. I didn't want to be split in two.

I stripped off my own jeans and boxers and tried not to look back at the group watching us as I went down on all fours.

Lila grabbed a tube of lube from the shelf and knelt down behind me. She squirted a ton of it on her fingers, then smeared it around my rear hole.

I shivered slightly. "That's cold."

She laughed softly. "Now you know how I feel."

I looked back at her and grinned. "Touché." I

dropped my head down as she slid a finger inside me.

"Is that okay?" she asked tentatively.

I was almost certain I could feel her fingers trembling. At the same time, they felt so fucking good. Gentle, but hot at the same time.

"That feels amazing," I replied. I swallowed hard as she slid in another finger, stretching me, readying me. Then a third.

The sensation of her filling me made my cock rock hard. I gripped myself and started to stroke slowly.

"Are you ready?" she asked.

"Yeah," I said, my voice hoarse. "Do it."

She gripped the sides of my ass and pressed the tip of the dildo into my slick, needy hole.

"Fuck," I groaned.

She stopped immediately. "Are you—"

"No, don't stop. It felt better than I thought it would." No wonder she was up for anal. It felt incredible.

"Okay." She pressed in deeper. Slowly. Determined not to hurt me. As if my queen could ever hurt me. Except in ways I liked to be hurt.

She slid in almost all the way before pulling back out again. "I almost wish I had an actual cock."

I laughed softly. "I almost wish you did too, but then you wouldn't be you."

"That's true." She thrust the dildo into me a few more times, then slid all the way out.

She unclicked the strap on and set it aside before lying down beside me and pulling her over me. She hooked her legs around my hips and pushed my cock down until I slid into her wet heat.

I groaned. "Fuck, this feels good too." I fucked her hard against the hardwood floor, driving my cock into her over and over. In no way was I as gentle with her as she was with me. She didn't want me to be.

"Fuck, Parker, just like that," she panted. "Ah, I'm going to…to come."

"Good girl, come around my cock," I told her. Her muscles clenched around me as she came, forcing an orgasm out of me too. I came hard into her, spilling my cum deep inside her luscious body.

I was barely down from my high when the lights went out, plunging us into total darkness.

CHAPTER 19

LILA

"Shit." I lay still, waiting for my body to come back down and the lights to turn back on.

The orgasm faded. The lights stayed off.

"We should figure out what the fuck is going on." Parker slid his cock out of me and patted around the floor before pressing my clothes into my hand. "Don't turn the light on your watch, in case something screwy is going on."

"Yeah," I agreed. The Academy's generator should have kicked in by now. Screwy was more likely than not. I dressed in about half a second. From the sounds beside me, he was doing the same.

He patted my back, then my arm before he found my hand and gripped it tight. "Stay with me. We'll be fine."

My heart raced like crazy. The bar wasn't a small

space and it wasn't silent, with everyone shuffling around. Trying to stay quiet, but audibly anxious at the same time.

I still felt enclosed. The only light was starlight that came through the window. It wasn't nearly enough to steady my nerves.

Before I stood, I felt around for something to use as a weapon. The only thing I could find was the strap on dildo, still slick with lube. It was better than nothing. I gripped it in my fist and let Parker pull me to my feet.

"Where are we going?" I whispered in his ear.

"We need to find—" he started to say.

A hand grabbed hold of my arm.. Without thinking, I let go of Parker and swung the dildo. I connected with something hard. The dildo striking with a thud.

"Fuck!" Hunter cried out. "Ouch."

"Shit, I'm sorry." I dropped the dildo to my side and searched around in the dark for Hunter.

He grunted. "What the hell did you hit me with? Wait, never mind. I don't think I want to know."

Parker chuckled. "What the hell is going on, bro?"

"No idea. Slade, where are you?" Hunter asked.

"Right behind you," Slade said softly. "I suggest you keep your voice down. Otherwise you might as well turn your phone on and announce your presence to everyone."

"Good idea," Hunter whispered. "Any idea which way Chloe and Dane went?

"I wasn't really keeping track," Slade admitted. "As soon as the lights went out, I headed in the direction I saw Lila last."

"Same dude, same," Hunter replied. "Lila doesn't like dark spaces. We need to get her out of here."

"That was what I was trying to do," Parker said. "I could use a weapon right now."

"I might have grabbed both of the tequila bottles," Slade said. "I can share."

"Perfect," Parker whispered. "If we get stuck in here, at least we can get shitfaced."

"Let's not get stuck in here." I was almost at the point where I'd prefer to give away our location than be in the dark any longer.

I shoved the thoughts away. I couldn't give into fear and paranoia. Whatever was going on, the darkness might ultimately prove to be our friend.

"The door is roughly that way," Hunter said. "We'll make our way over and see what happens from there."

"Bro, if you're pointing, we can't see you," Parker said.

"Oh, right. Everyone hold hands or some shit."

One of them gripped my left hand and another my right wrist.

"I hope that's Lila and not someone else," Parker said jokingly. His tone was light but his nerves were showing, even in the dark.

"It's me," I told him.

"Perfect." His hand slid down my wrist and felt around for what I was carrying. "Is that—"

"Yes," I said. "Yes it is. I would have grabbed a paddle or a flogger, but this was closer."

"At least it's not still warm," he said with a chuckle. He moved his hand back to my wrist and hung on carefully.

"It's fucking hard is what it is," Hunter said.

"I think that's the point," Slade said.

"Yeah, but you're not supposed to hit people over the head with it. Anyway, let's go. We'll go slowly. The last thing we want is to fall over furniture."

"Especially when Lila is carrying a hard dildo," Parker said. "That thing could put out someone's eye."

"You could console yourself with a bottle of tequila if that happens," Hunter told him.

"I think I'd need more than that." Parker walked behind me as Hunter led the way.

We stepped as silently and carefully as we could. Here and there, the shuffling continued. No one turned on a light. No one shouted or became hysterical. Every single person in that room knew there was a potential for them to become a target even though they didn't know who might be aiming.

At any normal university in Australia, everyone would have their phones out. They wouldn't even stop drinking or having a good time. But Brutham was a different place.

A dangerous fucking place.

Ahead of me came the thud of bodies connecting. That was followed by a short grunt of surprise from Hunter.

"Who the fuck is that?" he whispered.

"Dane DiMarco and Chloe," Dane said. "Is this some bullshit you assholes are pulling?"

Speaking of fucking dangerous.

"Funny, I was going to ask you the same thing," Hunter said. "We were right here with you. How could we have pulled anything?"

"Because you're you," Chloe said.

Hunter chuckled. "Thank you for the vote of confidence, but this isn't us. And if it isn't us, and it wasn't you, then—"

"It's someone else," I whispered. I remembered what Chloe said a couple of days ago about the twins having lots of enemies. His family, my family, none of us were short of enemies. Straight off the top of my head, I could think of several who might come after any one of us.

"Have you had any death threats recently, Mr D?" Parker asked.

"From anyone other than you guys? No," Dane replied. "You?"

"Same," Parker replied. "But that doesn't mean someone isn't after one of us in particular."

"That sounds like a good reason why we should stay away from them," Chloe said. "If whoever is behind this is after them, then we should make ourselves scarce."

"I was thinking the same about you," I said coldly. "Who else have you pissed off recently?"

She didn't answer.

"This might not be about any of us," Slade pointed out. "But whatever this is, we'll deal with it. We'll need weapons for that."

"I know where we can get some," Hunter said. "We need to get to them first."

"Yep, let's do that," Dane said. "But there are several hundred students and teachers here. Chances are, this has nothing to do with any of us."

He didn't sound like he believed his words either. Anyone with the last name Bell or Brantley, or with affiliations to either family, were going to be the prime targets. Most of the other students were from less influential families. Except those with ties to the Yakuza, Bratva or the Italian mafia.

Standing around contemplating the possibilities wasn't going to get us somewhere safe.

"We'll keep going," Hunter concluded. "We can't be far from the door."

We resumed walking, moving even more carefully now.

"There's the doorway," Hunter said. The corridor beyond that was bathed in moonlight.

That would make it easier to see but it would also make it easier to be seen.

"Where are we going?" I whispered.

"We need to get out of the building," Hunter said.

"They might be anticipating we'll do just that," Dane said. "We could be walking into an ambush."

"If they're outside waiting for us, they won't wait forever," Slade said. "Sooner or later, they'll come in after us. I don't know about you, but I prefer not to be a sitting duck. If we get out of the building, we can get what we need to fight back."

Dane grunted. "Fine, but if you get me or Chloe killed, I'm going to be pissed off with you, Lincoln."

"Right back at you, DiMarco," Slade said. "I don't suppose you have a gun on you?"

"If I did, I wouldn't tell you," Dane said.

Slade paused for a moment. "Yeah, I guess you wouldn't."

We stopped on the threshold.

"I don't like how bright that moonlight is," Hunter said. "If I was waiting to shoot someone, I'd be aiming a gun at that window there." He gestured. "The minute we step out, we'll be visible."

"So we don't step out," Slade said. "We keep down low, stay out of the moonlight and out of sight of anyone outside the window."

"Are you suggesting we crawl?" Parker asked.

"That's exactly what I'm suggesting," Slade said.

"Cool, I thought so," Parker said lightly. "I can get down on my hands and knees."

"We noticed, Park," Hunter said. "You seemed to enjoy it very much"

"I did, Hunt," Parker agreed. He knelt down, pulling me with him. "This would be easier without carrying a tequila bottle."

We kept our heads down and crawled toward the exit.

A glance back showed Hunter and Slade right behind me, Dane and Chloe behind them. She was sticking close to Dane; clearly scared, but I wasn't sure if she was scared of us or whatever the fuck else was going on. Both, perhaps? They were somewhat outnumbered.

I looked away. Right now, I needed to worry about getting myself and my guys out of here in one piece. Chloe and Dane could look after themselves.

We reached the doorway without getting shot or seeing anyone else. Either the other students had left the building, or they were hiding in their rooms, or somewhere else in the building. Wherever they were, we seemed to be the only ones moving around the corridor. What did that mean, if anything? Maybe nothing. Maybe everything.

I couldn't rule out the possibility everyone knew this was coming but us. Until I knew otherwise, I had to assume everyone but me and my guys were the enemy.

A million possibilities tumbled through my brain, none of them good. No one had ever, to my knowledge, attacked Brutham Academy. It never occurred to me before to wonder why that was. Considering who we all were, something like this was inevitable.

Of course it had to fucking happen when I was here.

"The minute we step out, we may become a target," Hunter whispered.

"Can you see anyone out there?" Dane asked. He crawled up beside Hunter and Parker.

"No one, but that doesn't mean they aren't there," Hunter said.

"What if someone goes out first?" Parker suggested.

"Are you volunteering?" Chloe asked him.

"Hell no," Parker replied. "Ladies first. And before you suggest Lila, remember you're the big sister."

"What if the first thing out isn't a person?" I held up the strap on with the bright pink dildo sticking out from the front.

"It's worth a try to see if we get a reaction," Hunter said.

I crawled over closer to the door, drew back my arm and threw the dildo as hard as I could.

CHAPTER 20

LILA

The dildo and strap landed on the ground with a plop. I waited with my breath held, but nothing happened.

"That was anticlimactic." Parker sounded disappointed. "I guess it's safe to go that way."

"Everyone wait here," Slade said. "I'll check it out first." He slipped past us and disappeared into the shadows.

"Assassin mode, activated," Parker said. "I need to learn me some skills like that."

"Just what the world needs," Hunter said. "Parker in stealth mode." His grin was a flash of white teeth in the dim light.

"Exactly," Parker agreed. "I'd be even more epic than I already am."

Chloe snorted.

Everyone's watches lit up simultaneously. Bathing us in light from a text message.

"Fuck." I cupped my hand around my watch to block the light while I quickly read.

> Brutham Academy alert, level five. All students shelter in place. Suspected incursion. More orders to follow

"Well, shit," Hunter said.

I pressed the crown on my watch to darken the screen. It would suck if a message meant to warn us, drew attention to us.

"It took them long enough," Dane said with a grunt. "We could have all been dead by now."

"Lucky for them, we're not," Parker said. After a moment he added, "Lucky for us too."

"That's a matter of opinion," Chloe muttered.

"My heart wouldn't break if you were dead," Parker told her. "But it seems like we might need each other to stay alive, so maybe we can stop being shit to each other for five minutes."

She gave him a scathing look but fell silent.

I peered out into the darkness. Every so often, I caught sight of a flash of light. Each time it was gone before I could pinpoint its location, but they seemed to be getting closer.

"There's at least a dozen out there," Slade said.

I jumped as he appeared in front of me suddenly. My heart thundered for a few moments, once it got going again.

"Fucking hell," Hunter whispered. "I need you to teach me that."

Slade gave him a quick glance, then said, "Follow me."

"How do we know we can trust you?" Chloe asked.

"You don't, but I don't want to end up dead," Slade told her. "You can follow me or you can stay here. That's your call."

"Personally, I'm not going to fuck around and find out," Hunter said. He put a hand on my lower back and moved forward slowly.

"Me either." Parker crawled along beside us until Slade gestured for us to stand.

"We're headed over to the sheds," Slade whispered. "If that text message was right, we will need those weapons."

I assumed by supplies, he meant guns. I'd feel better if we were armed with more than a couple of tequila bottles.

We kept to the side of the steps, where shadows were deepest, and moved down in single file. I winced as our footsteps crunched on the gravel at the front of the building. Each step sounded like a clap of thunder.

I stepped past the dildo and considered scooping it up. If only so I had something in my hand to defend myself with. I dismissed the idea. Even if I moved quickly, I'd be stepping out of the shadows into the moonlight. The risk of being seen was too great.

Slade led us off the gravel and onto grass, where our footsteps were muffled. We made it to a line of trees before the lights converged on the Academy building. Slade was right, there were about a dozen of them. Dark silhouettes with a phone or torch in one hand and a gun in the other.

"They don't look like they're here for a party," Parker whispered. "Chloe, are you sure they're not with you?"

"If they were, I would have told them where to find you by now," she pointed out.

"And if they were with us, we would have done the same," I said. "Chances are, they want both of us dead."

"Zachary looked pissed off the last time we saw him," Parker said. "They could be friends of his."

"I'm starting to think Zachary is unhinged," Hunter said. "That's saying something, given the company I keep."

"You can't see me right now, but I'm flipping you off," Parker told him.

"Let's keep going," Dane said.

"The more distance we put between us and them, the better." Slade led the way through the trees, somehow moving silently over the dry leaves.

"Make a note of the date," Parker said. "Mr D and Slade agreeing on something."

"We can all agree we don't want to die," Hunter said.

"Can we all agree that you should shut up?" Chloe snapped.

"I actually think that's a good idea," I said. "In the interests of not ending up dead."

Parker muttered something under his breath but the twins fell silent until we reached the sheds.

We stopped in the shadows about twenty metres away and watched.

"This isn't an inside job," Dane said softly.

"No," Slade said. "Unless they don't know what's kept in the sheds."

"That's possible," Dane conceded. "But if that's the case, they didn't do their homework."

"Either way, they're not—" Slade was interrupted by the sound of gunshots. Someone screamed. Another shouted, but that was cut short by another gunshot.

"We need to hurry." Slade trotted over to one of the sheds and pulled out a set of keys from his pocket. He slid one into the lock and opened the door.

The walls of the shed were lined with guns, ammunition, flame throwers, bats and what looked like a rocket launcher.

Hunter rubbed his hands together. "I love this place." He went straight for the rocket launcher.

"Trying to overcompensate?" Chloe asked.

"Sweetheart, I'm the only one with big enough muscles to pick this thing up." He grinned.

She rolled her eyes at him and grabbed up a handgun. I took the one beside it.

I thought Parker might opt for a flamethrower, because why not? Instead, he picked up a handgun of his own. But only after opening the tequila bottle and taking a swig.

"Now it's a party." He grinned.

Dane picked up a handgun for himself, hesitated for a moment then grabbed another. "Can never be too careful."

"Hey," a whisper came from the doorway.

I aimed my gun, but lowered it when I saw Tina and Angie.

"Looks like we weren't the only ones who thought

to come here." Tina stepped past us and picked up a weapon of her own.

"Definitely not." Zachary entered next, followed by another handful of students.

"This went from a party to a battle," Parker remarked. "The battle for Brutham Academy." He put a fist to his chest. "They can take our school over our cold, dead bodies."

Chloe made a derisive sound in the back of her throat. "They can have the fucking school. I just want to get out of here alive."

"Me too," I agreed. Loyalty was one thing, getting killed to save our school was another. "Zachary, those aren't friends of yours?"

"I was going to ask the same question," he replied. "I thought you might be getting desperate, so you called in reinforcements."

"Nope, nothing to do with us," I said. "I guess this means we're on the same side, for now." If that was what it took to get out of this alive, then I'd do it. But I wouldn't turn my back on him or Chloe. Vice versa, no doubt.

"What's the plan?" Dane asked Slade. "Do we take them on or get the fuck out of here?" He winced at the sound of another few gunshots.

"You can get the fuck out of here if you want,"

Slade said. "I'm not going to stand by and let them kill everyone in the school."

"That's noble, but you might get yourself killed," Dane said.

Slade shrugged one muscular shoulder. "I'm not that easy to kill. Are you? Imagine the gratitude you'll get from the students' families."

Dane considered for a moment, then aimed his gun at Zachary's head. "Did you drug Chloe?"

Zachary didn't flinch. "No, I promise I did not. The twin assholes engineered that."

"Guilty," Parker said. "Now, are we going to stand here talking or are we going to go and kill some motherfuckers?"

"We could kill some motherfuckers right now," Dane said. He swivelled his upper body and aimed at Parker's head.

"Pull the trigger and we'll find out how well a rocket launcher works at close range," Hunter warned.

I sighed. "You all have big cocks, okay? Let's go before there's no one left alive."

I turned and stepped toward the doorway. I half expected to hear shots behind me, but I didn't. A few grunts of dissatisfaction, but then everyone filed out behind me.

"Men."

I glanced over to see Chloe walking beside me. I actually managed a half-smile.

"We can't really blame them for not trusting each other," I said. "We haven't been very good role models in that department."

"If you're trying to—" she started.

"I'm not trying to do anything," I whispered. "Just stay alive. After that, we can go back to being at each other's throats."

She didn't answer for a minute or two. "I'm not going to let myself get killed to convenience you, just so you know."

I laughed softly. "Me either. I wouldn't want to disappoint you by taking that away from you. I'm sure you'd prefer the satisfaction of killing me yourself."

"Exactly," she replied. "I'm sure you're thinking the same thing about me."

What I was actually thinking was, how did we get to this point? When everything was said and done, she was still my twin sister. We must have been close once. Maybe before we were born. I was almost certain neither of us tried to loop an umbilical cord around the other's throat.

I grimaced. If Dad was here, he'd probably tell me that was exactly what I should have done. If I had, it would have changed every aspect of my life. What would it have been like growing up without my twin? Boring, at worst.

"Just don't go getting yourself killed tonight, okay?" I said.

"Yeah, you too," she whispered.

If I didn't know better, I'd think she was being sentimental. I couldn't think about that right now. Even if she was, it didn't change anything. Once we dealt with this, the competition would continue and things would get brutal. Right now, I had to focus on tonight and getting through this with me and my guys intact.

We kept to the shadows, moving as silently as a group of about fifteen people could. Granted, all of us were trained for things like this. To fight, to kill.

Chloe and I had handled guns since before we could walk. I had no doubt Hunter knew exactly how to use a fucking rocket launcher. If anyone could, it would be him. And he'd laugh while doing it. That was all kinds of fucked up, but I loved it.

Gunshots rang out again from inside the Academy building. A couple of people shouted. The sound of running footsteps was cut short by another shot.

"It sounds like they're hunting them down," Slade said. His voice was ice cold fury. That was sexy as hell. Hearing him sound so protective made the pulse in my clit pound harder.

"At the risk of sounding cliché, the hunter just became the prey." Hunter brandished the rocket launcher. "And this Hunter loves nothing more than a good hunt."

"It's not fair that you got a cooler name than I did," Parker told him.

"When this is over, you can change your name to Tracker, if you want," Hunter said.

"Hmmm, I'll think about it." Parker didn't sound convinced.

Slade shook his head at him, gripped his gun in both hands and started up the steps.

CHAPTER 21
PARKER

I kept close to Lila as we moved through the corridors. Every now and again, a shot would ring out, or a scream or shout would come from somewhere else in the building. They'd only last for a second or two before fading into silence again. That made it difficult to pin down the exact location of the attackers. They seemed to be moving through the building, some on the bottom floor, some on the second.

"Someone get the—" a voice shouted from up ahead. Whatever else he said, I couldn't make it out. He was definitely only ten or fifteen metres ahead of us. This part of the school contained the classrooms. At a guess, they were in one of the chemistry labs.

"This way," Slade whispered. "There has to be at least two of them in there."

"This wasn't what we were sent here for," a second voice said.

"Who cares?" said a third. "We can just... Did you hear something?"

Slade lunged toward the doorway, Hunter and I on his heels. Zachary and Dane weren't far behind.

Slade was illuminated by the light from the attackers. He raised his gun and fired.

A grunt and a thud said he hit his mark. He ducked sideways, narrowly missing return fire.

I got off a couple of shots. The first missed, but the second took an attacker right in the stomach. He cried out in pain and doubled over before falling to the floor.

The next thing I knew, Zachary was standing shoulder to shoulder with me, taking out the third asshole with a neat shot right through the centre of his forehead.

"Dude, nice shot." I didn't like the guy, but I had to give him credit. It was a better shot than mine.

"I have skills." Zachary shrugged.

Dane stepped into the room and ended the moaning of the guy shot in the stomach. A shot to the left side of his chest left the room in a few moments of silence.

"Three down, nine to go," Hunter said.

"What exactly are you going to do with that thing?" I ask him. "You can't use it without destroying half the school."

"It's a last resort," he told me. "If I have to decimate the place to get rid of the infestation of invaders, that's what I'll do."

"You've been watching too many science-fiction movies," Dane told him.

Hunter grinned. "There's no such thing as too many." He grabbed one of the attacker's guns and held it in his hand while he slung the rocket launcher over his shoulder. "For the record, it's shows like *Firefly* and *Stargate*. Not to mention *Buffy the Vampire Slayer*."

"Yeah, well don't get us killed by doing stuff that works on TV," Dane said.

"I'll try my best, but I make no promises," Hunter said. "Where to next?"

"We wait a couple of minutes," Slade said. "The noise we just made won't go unnoticed. They may come to us."

"Better than coming on us," I quipped.

"I'd prefer cum to bullets," Lila said.

I smiled at her and draped an arm over her shoulders.

"Me too, babe, me too." I loved the idea that this

was going down while she was still sticky with mine. I definitely wanted to try that strap on dildo thing with her again. That felt incredible. And probably the closest I'd ever come to having a cock in my ass.

"Down this way," someone in the corridor called out.

We pressed ourselves back against the walls, keeping flat in the shadows. Without knowing if the approaching footsteps belonged to friend or foe, we held a collective breath and waited.

"Clark?" A male voice asked. "Calzone?"

Absolutely not friends. I frowned, trying to gauge who sent them. They were common enough names that they didn't stand out in my memory.

After what happened in Vancouver with Abbie and Wolf Venom, the Fiorelli family were still more or less in disarray. I couldn't rule out the possibility of their involvement. If that was the case, it was probably Hunter and me they were after. Hunter killed the family's eldest daughter. I've never known a Fiorelli to be particularly forgiving.

Lights flickered in the corridor. A phone or a torch being shone this way and that. Finally, it shone through the doorway into the lab.

"In—" He never got that word out before a bullet slammed into the side of his head, courtesy of Slade.

He barely hit the ground when four more took his place.

They first shot wildly. A couple of bullets hitting a shelf of bottles right behind me, igniting the contents.

"Fuck." I pulled Lila down to the floor with me. "That almost singed my hair."

"No one singes my brother's hair but me," Hunter declared before shooting the asshole in the hand. Then in the chest for good measure.

"Thanks for defending my hair, bro," I called out.

"Any time, bro," he replied.

The other two attackers ducked to either side of the door.

"We have the Academy surrounded." One spoke in an accent I couldn't quite identify. "There's no way out."

"I hate to break it to you, but that's very much untrue," Hunter said. "Also, if I was you, I'd leave while I was still alive. Just some friendly words of advice. I don't expect you to listen."

"The fucking Brantley twins," the attacker growled. "I'm particularly looking forward to killing you two."

"Will you do us the courtesy of telling us who sent you before you kill us?" Hunter asked. "It seems like the least you can do."

"Fuck off," the attacker called back. "I'm not telling you shit."

"Mercenaries," Slade said. "They're not telling because they don't know. They just got paid to come here and kill."

"It's a nice job if you can get it," I remarked. "But a cop out. Whoever sent them is trying to send a message. If we don't know who that is, how are we going to know what the message is meant to be?"

"No message." He sounded Italian. "Just your death."

"Hey, Dane." I squinted into the shadows, roughly in the direction I thought he was.

"What?" Dane asked.

"You said Hunter watches too many movies. What about these guys?" They were about as melo-dramatic as you could get.

Dane grunt-laughed. "Yeah, sounds like they watch too many of them too."

"Get the others down here," an Italian-voice snapped to someone, presumably speaking into his phone. "Last chance to give yourselves up."

"Oh?" Hunter said. "We didn't realise that was an option. Are you saying if we step out of here, you won't kill us?"

"No, but we might consider killing you quicker," Italian-voice said.

"No deal," Lila said. In my ear she whispered, "We need a distraction."

"We could use an exploding teddy bear right about now," I whispered back.

"We have something better," Zachary whispered.

He slipped over to a cupboard at the side of the room and started doing something I couldn't see. It sounded like he was pouring the contents of one bottle into another. That was followed by the sound of fabric ripping.

He held a bottle with a scrap of his T-shirt sleeve hanging out the top, up to the shelf which still burnt slightly. When the fabric ignited, he hurled the bottle out into the corridor.

The glass shattered, sending liquid and glass everywhere. The liquid ignited and exploded in a flash of flame and a bang loud enough to make my ears ring.

One of the attackers screamed in pure agony. He ran past the doorway, his clothes engulfed in flames.

"Ouch," I remarked. "That wouldn't tickle." I didn't want to be impressed with Zachary, but once again, I was. An impromptu explosive was impressive.

The corridor flooded with smoke thick enough to make my eyes sting. A second or two later, the smoke alarms sounded, deafeningly loud. That was followed by the sprinkler system kicking in and spraying us all with a torrent of water.

"This isn't how I like to get wet," Lila said.

"Me either. We need to get out of here," Slade said. "Everyone will know where we are by now."

"Time for the rocket launcher?" Hunter looked hopeful.

"There's a door at the other end of the corridor," Dane said. "We can head down there and wait for the rest of them."

Slade nodded. "Let's do it." He stepped toward the doorway carefully. Peered out. "I can't see anyone." He gestured for us all to move out.

Tina and Angie stepped out into the corridor first, guns raised. A shot rang out, then another. The first took Tina right between the eyes. The second slammed into Angie's chest.

"Fuck." Slade looked stricken as they fell to the floor. He stepped out, aimed and shot off several bullets.

Turns out a grunt of pain sounds the same in an Italian accent. Especially when it comes to an abrupt end.

"Motherfucker." Slade lowered his gun before gesturing again. "Come on."

I helped Lila to her feet and steered her out of the room. Her expression when she looked down at the bodies of the two other women was grim. Slade was going to beat himself up about that, no doubt.

The Italian asshole must have been hiding in another classroom, waiting to see what we'd do. He could just as easily have been killed in Zachary's explosion. The misjudgement was unfortunate, but not Slade's fault. I made a mental note to tell him that later. Whether or not it would make a difference was another thing.

We reached the door at the end of the corridor and ducked down low to wait. All of us had weapons raised, ready. Dane had a gun in each hand, looking like a character from a computer game. Ironic given how quick he was to judge us for watching TV shows and movies.

I never would have picked him for a gamer, but then again I barely knew the guy. He could be a furry for all I know. Probably a dog, or maybe a bilby. That mental image almost made me laugh out loud. Nothing against the lifestyle, I just couldn't really picture Dane doing that.

I tilted my head back and let the sprinkler wash the smoke out of my eyes.

I took a moment to glance at Lila, who looked hot as fuck in dripping wet clothes. She looked hot as fuck in and out of everything, but the way her clothes clung to her body made my balls heavy.

Yeah, when were they not heavy? Especially around her. Especially when the fabric was all but transparent, her nipples visible as peaks in the cotton. I wanted to close my lips around one of them and suck.

I shook droplets of my face and focused my attention back up the corridor. If I let myself be too distracted, I could get her killed. No one would ever forgive me if that happened, including me.

The sprinklers shut off, leaving us in damp silence, except the sound of dripping, which gradually slowed. Clearly the electricity was still running to the building, or the sprinklers wouldn't have worked. The assholes must have messed with the fuse box to shut off the lights.

For mercenaries, they seemed to know what they were doing. They'd planned this in advance. They must have if they knew where the fuse box was. Although, they'd missed the weapons shed. Or had they? The more I thought about it, the less sense this made.

Who the hell had the time and money to send dickheads like this after us? It must have cost a small fortune. Who was so desperate they'd bother? We were hard to kill, but there were easier, cheaper methods than this.

I caught Lila in the corner of my eye as she turned her head.

"Fuck," she whispered.

"What is it?" A second later, I realised our mistake. Half a second before the door behind us opened and gunshots rang out again.

CHAPTER 22
PARKER

Hunter raised the rocket launcher. He pointed it at the four attackers.

"Die motherfuckers!" He pressed the trigger. It clicked but nothing happened.

"Fuck." He gripped it in two hands and smashed it into the head of the nearest attacker. The man went down with a cry of pain.

Hunter threw the rocket launcher aside and pulled out his gun to finish the job.

I put myself between the assholes and Lila, while at the same time shoving her back up the corridor.

The last three attackers surged inside the building. One of them took aim at Zachary. He ducked aside at the last moment and the bullet hit one of his friends in the chest.

I took the opportunity to shoot that guy in the

head. The attacker, not Zachary, tempting though that was.

A second later, pain and heat passed through my shoulder. It took another few seconds to register I'd been shot. It wasn't much more than a graze, but it hurt like a bitch.

"Parker, are you okay?" Lila stepped out from behind me, barely glanced at me before putting a bullet in the chest of the guy who shot me.

"I am now," I said approvingly. She killed a guy for me, what could be hotter than that?

The last attacker turned and ran, but Dane put a bullet between his shoulder blades. He flew forward and slammed into the floor.

Silence fell, heavy and oppressive.

"Are we sure that's the last of them?" Chloe asked finally.

"I wouldn't assume anything," Lila said. "Not yet." She was wet and tired, but her chin was raised. If this was only the beginning, she'd keep fighting.

"Everyone hunker down," Slade said. "I'm going to take a look around outside."

"I'll go with you," Dane said.

Slade regarded him for a moment, then nodded. "Fine. Everyone else, stay here." They moved slowly towards the door and slipped out into the night.

I pulled off my shirt and pressed it to my shoulder.

Lila put a hand over mine to help hold the fabric in place. "That looks painful."

I started to shrug but stopped and winced. "I've had worse." I nodded towards the dead bodies lying on the floor. "I'm better off than them."

"That's true," she said. "We still need to get you to—"

The lights flickered and came back on.

I blinked against the sudden glare.

The floor of the corridor was covered with a combination of blood and water. It looked like a literal bloodbath. Here and there, bullet holes dotted the walls. I didn't *think* they'd been there before. No doubt they'd be patched up by the end of the week like they were never there.

The attackers all lay dead, each dressed entirely in black. Unless I was mistaken, none would carry ID, or anything to indicate who they were and who hired them. They were nothing more now than nameless, faceless mercenaries. Which was just how guys like them liked it.

"What a mess." Hunter clicked his tongue. "I hope they don't expect us to clean that up." He glanced over at me and realised I was injured. "Didn't duck fast enough?" He grinned.

"Fuck off," I said cheerfully. "I love you too, bro."

He laughed. "It's just another scar. You'll live. This time."

"Just trying to make it easier to tell us apart," I said lightly. As if my crooked nose didn't do that already. Although, statistically speaking, chances were Hunter would get punched in the nose at some point. It might even be someone other than me that did it.

Hunter patted my other shoulder. "Keep telling yourself that." He peered towards the window. "We should go and hide. There's a couple of cars approaching."

I looked in the same direction. Two black cars were headed up the driveway, both illuminated in the blazing lights at the front of the Academy building.

"What the hell?" Lila's face paled.

"What is it?" I asked.

It was Chloe who answered. "That's Dad's car. What the hell is he doing here?" She glanced over at Zachary, who shook his head.

"I have no idea," he admitted.

I squinted as the cars came to a stop outside the building. "This gets weirder and weirder. That looks like Reuben's car."

"It really fucking does," Hunter said. "I'm going to go out there and see."

"I'm coming with you," I told him.

I turned to say something to Lila, but she was already halfway out the door, Chloe right behind her.

"I guess we're all going," I said to myself. "What could possibly go wrong?"

My hand pressed hard against my shoulder, I headed out the door and down the steps.

Both of the cars were parked side-by-side. Reuben stood leaning against one, his arms crossed over his chest.

Samuel Bell stood beside the other in a similar pose. His brown eyes took in his daughters and Zachary as they stepped out of the building together.

For someone who would happily see Samuel Bell dead, Reuben had a remarkably similar expression on his face when he looked at Hunter and me. Although, where Samuel looked slightly disappointed, Reuben looked disapproving.

"You're alive, I see," Samuel drawled.

"You were expecting to come here and find us dead?" Hunter asked.

"I was hopeful you might be," Samuel told him. His gaze swung back to Lila and Chloe. "You survived this little test."

Lila sucked in a breath.

Time stopped while we all stared at him, trying to absorb what he just said.

"Little test?" Lila finally choked out. "You sent those mercenaries to attack the Academy?"

Samuel looked remarkably unapologetic. "The school board agreed that if I bankrolled another trial, it could take place." He tilted his head slightly towards Reuben.

I looked back at my older brother. His expression was unchanged. I should have guessed he and Samuel were behind this. Who else would be twisted enough?

"I guess we passed," I said lightly. "We didn't die. That sounds like a pass to me, right Hunt?"

"Right, Park," Hunter agreed. He looked like he wanted to pick up the rocket launcher, figure out why it didn't work the first time and use it on Samuel and Reuben. Failing that, he might pick up the dildo where it still lay on the ground and hit them over the head with it.

Pissed didn't even begin to describe it.

Lila looked even more furious. "You sent people to kill us? Who does that?"

Samuel ignored the question. "You four worked together?"

"Just this once," Chloe snapped. "Don't worry, it won't happen again."

"Definitely not," Lila agreed. "I can't believe you'd do something like this. What sort of monster—"

Samuel exhaled out his nose. "I was hoping this test would toughen you up. Make you reassess your priorities. Instead, it seems to have done the opposite. I'm starting to think none of you should take my place."

Lila must have remembered she was holding a gun, because she raised it slowly and pointed it at her father.

"You sent people to kill us," she said again.

"Did you die?" he said evenly. He actually seemed pleased she had a gun aimed at his head.

"She could have," I said, barely containing my rage.

"We all could have," Hunter added. "Those assholes could have killed everyone in the school. Even if they had orders not to kill Chloe and Lila, it was dark in there. It's only skill and us working together that prevented that from happening."

Reuben rolled his eyes.

Samuel settled his gaze on Hunter. "There was no such order. Just like there is no such order during the trials. If my daughters don't have the skills to get through this, then they won't survive in the long run."

"You're a special kind of asshole," I told him. He didn't seem to give a shit Lila could be dead right now because of him. I turned to Reuben. "You too. The trials are one thing. Armed mercenaries are another."

The sides of Reuben's mouth twitched. "Nothing you couldn't handle. Don't tell me you didn't enjoy yourselves."

I opened my mouth. Closed it again. The fucker was right, we had enjoyed it. It was exactly the kind of shit we got off on. And he fucking knew that too.

"I thought so." He nodded faintly. "They haven't nicknamed this place Brutal Academy for nothing. You should all be able to handle situations like this with one hand tied behind your back. As far as I'm concerned, this test was a success."

Samuel frowned at him. "We'll have to agree to disagree."

"Were you hoping one of us would die so you don't have to think too hard anymore?" Lila asked. "Or two of us." She jerked her head in Zachary's direction.

"Not at all," Samuel replied. "I was hoping this would make you fight harder for what you want. I was hoping to see one of you handle the situation better than the others."

"Lila used a dildo as an improvised weapon," I

said helpfully. "And Hunter is handy with a rocket launcher. It was kinda epic." I couldn't stop a smile from creeping onto my lips.

"Zachary is an amazing shot," Hunter said. "Slade and Dane too." He glanced around for them. "And Zachary made a bomb. That was cool." He was almost smiling now too.

"Chloe held her own," Zachary argued. "She was amazing."

Samuel looked unimpressed. "Next time, I expect to see you all perform better."

"Next time?" Lila echoed. Her hand was steady. She didn't seem to have made up her mind about whether to use the gun on her father or not.

I could understand her conflict. This might be part of the test too. Part of me wanted her to go ahead and kill him, but she'd hate herself for it later. She wanted him to approve of her and choose her, not take his place by killing him. Personally, I think killing him would be a lot easier, but it wasn't my call to make.

"There will always be a next time," Samuel said. "It might be at the trials and it might be before that. Or after. You need to be on your guard against anything and everything. Always. That is the point of tonight's test. To remind you of that. You can never become complacent. Not for a minute, not for an hour, not for a day. The moment you do, someone will work their way under your armour and get to you."

"Like sneaking into your house and putting a virus on your computer?" I asked.

He barely glanced at me. "Like that, yes. That could have been much worse than it was. We have to be ready for every contingency. It could come from anyone." Now he looked at me. Accusingly.

"Nothing would ever make me go after Lila," I said firmly. "She can totally trust me, Hunter and Slade." After a moment I added, "Has anyone told you you have trust issues?"

He actually twitched. Apparently I hit on a raw nerve. Interesting. Who would have the guts to tell him something like that, apart from me? Instinct told me there was a woman involved. I didn't know why they did, but they did. I filed that away for later. You never know when information like that could come in useful.

"I should be on my way," Samuel said. "I'm sure you're wanting to get some rest after the excitement." He made it sound like we'd had a party or something. As if there weren't fuck only knew how many dead bodies lying inside the Academy.

"Just remember," he added as he opened the door to his car, "Don't let your guard down." He nodded to his daughters, then slipped inside and closed the door behind him.

It was Hunter who took the gun from Lila's hand and put his arms around her.

"That was some fucked up shit," he remarked.

None of us disagreed.

CHAPTER 23

LILA

I stewed on my father's words while we trudged back into the building. Staff and teachers appeared from wherever they'd been hiding, and started to clean up the corridors. None of them looked horrified or even surprised.

"This is all kinds of screwy," Hunter said.

"Yeah," was all I managed to say. My brain was overloaded with the attempt to understand everything.

I knew this year was going to be a challenge, but I didn't expect anything like this. I certainly didn't expect my father to send people into the school to kill. The problem was, I *should* have expected it. This was my father we were talking about. Whenever anyone describes the Bell family, they use the words 'the worst of the worst.' I didn't really stop to contemplate what that meant before now.

Apparently what it meant was killing your children if they don't meet your expectations.

What was his expectation anyway? I was supposed to tell Chloe and Zachary to stay put somewhere safe while I dealt with twelve armed assailants? Was I supposed to tell the twins to stay out of it?

Slade trotted up to us as we headed out of the Academy hospital. The doctor had patched up Parker. He hadn't even needed stitches, just a bandage and a warning to take it easy for a while. As if Parker knew how to take it easy.

"It's all clear out there. Was that your father I saw driving away?" Slade slowed to a walk beside us.

Hunter explained everything to him. He sounded as overwhelmed as I felt. Not to mention conflicted. I knew he and Parker had enjoyed themselves. Hunter was in his element carrying a rocket launcher around the school. The twins motto seemed to be 'enjoy life to the fullest.' If they died tonight, at least they'd look and feel good doing it.

That wouldn't be much consolation for me, if they were dead.

Slade's eyes widened with disgust. "Twelve mercenaries and at least ten students are dead. For what? So your father could play his stupid fucking games?"

I tried not to bristle. Instinctively, I felt like I should defend him, even though what he did was indefensible. He was my father and what he did was only to make me stronger.

I just wished he'd... find a better way to go about it.

"He—" I couldn't think of a single thing to say, so I shook my head. "You're right, it was fucked up. He did it because he doesn't think I'm strong enough. If I was, none of this would have happened."

"Hey." Hunter stepped around in front of me and put his hands on my shoulders to stop me. "This is not your fault. If he can't see how strong you are, then he's not looking close enough."

"Isn't he?" I said bitterly. "Maybe you're biased. Maybe the whole point of tonight was that I was supposed to take charge of the Academy. Hell, maybe I was supposed to take charge of *mercenaries* and hunt down Chloe."

I shook my head. "Either of those would have been better than protecting her and Zachary. Or letting Zachary protect us."

"I'm not saying hunting down Chloe with a bunch of mercenaries wouldn't have been fun," Hunter said slowly. "But that's not who you are. You had to protect yourself. Those assholes could have been after you. If you'd tried to take charge of them, they could have killed you. Or worse."

That reminded me of Danica and Mary. I didn't want to think what twelve men might do to me.

I shuddered.

"You couldn't have known your father was involved," Slade said. "If you had, you would have behaved differently."

"Would I?" I asked.

"Yeah," Parker agreed. "You would have called him up and told him to call off his dogs. Then we could have gone back and finished our game of Kink or Drink."

I groaned, remembering we'd only just started when the lights went out. Zachary trying to make Chloe jealous by choking Tina seemed so ridiculously childish now. Okay, it was childish then, but it was even more so now with twenty-two people dead.

"I suppose I would have," I agreed. "But he wouldn't have listened. They would still have come after us. If we knew he was behind it, we would have assumed they had orders not to kill Chloe or me. We might have hesitated."

"If we had, we'd be dead right now," Slade said. "None of us hesitated. We did what had to be done. If your father doesn't like it, too fucking bad. What matters is that we survived."

"Except Tina, Angie and fuck knows who else," I said. "This had nothing to do with any of them. Dad would call them collateral damage." Just like Mary.

"That's exactly what Reuben would say," Hunter said. "He probably got a good laugh out of all of this."

"Reuben laughs?" I asked dryly.

Hunter grinned. "Not out loud. He smiles once in a while though. Very rarely and usually when things have gone horribly wrong for someone else."

"That sounds like Reuben." I grabbed Hunter's wrists and pushed him a few steps back to my door.

"Right now, I want a nice, hot shower and to get out of these damp clothes." I let his wrists go and pulled out my key.

Tentatively I slipped it into the lock and turned it. The door opened easily. My room looked untouched. The sprinklers hadn't come on in this part of the Academy, thank fuck. Otherwise everything I owned would be saturated.

So would everything the guys owned. We'd have to leave and find a hotel for a few days. We could do that anyway.

I won't lie, that was a tempting thought, but I

wasn't going to run. Whatever Chloe, Zachary or my father threw at me, I would deal with it.

Slade placed his hands on my shoulders and steered me into the room and towards the bathroom. We stopped at the threshold for him to pull my T-shirt over my head. He unhooked my bra and slid the wet lace down my arms.

Hunter started on my shorts while Parker turned on the shower.

A girl could get used to this. I couldn't say they didn't take good care of me. They called me their queen and treated me like one.

I stepped under the hot spray, surrounded by three even hotter, naked guys.

Parker stood with his shoulder raised, out of the water. It looked sore, but the bullet only grazed his skin. A few centimetres to the right, and he'd be dead.

I may not have hesitated to shoot my father if Parker died because of his fucking games. Screwing with me was one thing. Killing one of my guys was unforgivable.

Besides that, the whole attack could have led to me, Chloe and Zachary all dying. What would Dad have done then? Hunt down someone like Hades Turner to take his place? Or maybe he had something else in mind. He wasn't too old to have more children. I knew he wasn't sentimental, but this...

"Put it out of your head for a while," Hunter said. "We got through it. Everything they've thrown at us, we've survived. That's the important thing." He massaged my shoulders with his fingers and scented body wash.

"What he said." Slade squirted body wash onto his hands and started washing my breasts and stomach. "Also, we wouldn't let anything happen to you."

"No way." Parker washed himself quickly, then pushed Hunter aside to wash my hair.

"You know I can do this for myself, right?" I asked.

"We like doing it for you," Parker said.

Slade knelt down in front of me and washed my thighs carefully before he parted them to press his face between my legs. "You can't do this yourself." He traced a circle around my clit with his tongue.

I shivered. "That's true, I can't." I wouldn't want to. Having them lick me was much more fun.

Hunter rinsed himself off and stood to the side to run hot, wet hands over my breasts. He pinched my nipples gently, then more firmly.

Parker placed his hands to either side of my chin and tilted my head back to help him rinse my hair.

I closed my eyes and let the hot water rush down the back of my head and over my face.

"You're spoiling me."

"Yes, and we're going to keep on spoiling you," Parker told me.

"Yes we are," Hunter agreed. He leaned down to kiss my nipple with his tongue, before drawing it into his mouth and sucking. "You always taste so good."

"It's the body wash," I said.

He laughed. "No, it's definitely you. Nothing ever tasted as good as this."

"Or this." Slade licked my clit firmly, kissing and nibbling while running his thumbs up and down the insides of my thighs. "This tastes like heaven."

"It feels like heaven." I grabbed one of Parker's hands and squeezed tightly as I rocked my hips back and forth on Slade's mouth.

My other hand slid down to grip Hunter's erect cock. He was slick with water and hot and hard with need. I slid my hand from his head to his balls slowly, carefully. I didn't want him to finish too quickly.

He thrust into my hand, just as slowly. "I will never get enough of you touching me," he said. "You always feel so incredible. So fucking perfect."

"No, you three are so fucking perfect," I told them.

I leaned back against Parker as I came hard. I wanted to scream all of their names at once, but all I could manage was a shout toward the ceiling.

I was just coming down when Slade stood. He gripped my ass and picked me up until my legs wrapped around his waist. With one thrust, he slid me onto his cock. Between him and Parker, they held my slippery, wet body. Slade started to pound into me with even, almost frantic thrusts.

If anything gave away his state of mind after the attack, it was this. He was more scared than he let on. For him, for me, for the twins. For all of us. He needed to let off steam and remind me, and himself, that we were still alive.

In spite of that, he didn't come quickly. He was so in control of himself he managed to keep himself from coming even when he was clearly right on the edge. His breathing was ragged with desire and exertion, his need great.

Finally, he gave in and let his orgasm claim him. Hunter came a moment later, squirting hot cum all over my hand.

I could have washed it off under the water, but instead I let his cock go and brought his hand to my mouth. My eyes on his, I licked his pearly release from my palm and fingers.

"Now this is delicious," I told him. Thick, salty

and warm. With the slightest hint of his own personal flavour.

"Woman, you are next level hot," Hunter told me. "I'm starting to think we should run away and hide out somewhere."

I laughed softly. "Don't tempt me." A secluded island far away from the Academy, my sister, my father, Zachary and next week's exam, sounded like bliss. The exam in particular was something I'd love to avoid as long as I could. Yeah, that's how much I hate exams. Priorities.

"Let's get out." Parker turned off the water. He helped me slide off Slade's cock and back onto the floor. He stepped out and handed me a towel. "Get nice and dry on the outside. I intend to keep you nice and wet on the inside." He grinned and grabbed a towel for himself.

"Did I mention you're spoiling me?" I teased.

"Babe, we've only just started spoiling you," Hunter said.

"They're right," Slade said. "There's a lot more where that came from and we're going to give you every bit of it."

CHAPTER 24

LILA

"He's right, you know." Chloe flopped down on the chair beside me.

"Who is?" I barely glanced away from my laptop screen. I should have chosen somewhere more private to study than the library, but after the attack I didn't want to be alone.

Sleeping at night without having nightmares was hard enough.

"Dad." She leaned forward and rested her elbows on the top of the table. "What he said about not doing enough."

"Are you suggesting I'm not doing enough?" I closed my laptop and swivelled around in my seat to look at her. "Should I strangle you now and get it over with?"

She rolled her eyes. "No. I mean our first instincts

should have been to turn the attack to our advantage. Not team up and run."

"We fought back," I pointed out. "We could have hidden in the bush until it was all over. We didn't."

"No, but if we were thinking right, one of us would insisted the other go and hide. If I dealt with it while you were trembling under a tree, I would have won."

I smirked. "If my guys and I went and trembled under a tree, you'd be dead and Zachary with you."

"Then neither of us would have won. Dad isn't going to let a coward take his place." She chewed on the tip of a bright pink nail.

"You got that vibe too?" When she gave me a questioning look, I added, "I got the impression he has a plan for none of us to take over. Like somehow all of this is a test he wants us to fail."

"Why would he want that?" She narrowed her eyes at me, but didn't deny the suggestion.

I considered for a moment, but slowly shook my head. "I don't know. I'm starting to get the impression nothing we can do will be enough for him."

"He is Dad," she pointed out. "When have we ever been enough for him? Maybe if we were born with cocks, he'd be more satisfied. Or if Zachary's mother gave him a little boy."

"That would have pissed Zachary off." I smiled. "Passed over for his own half brother."

Chloe frowned. "We would have been passed over for the same little half brother."

"Yeah, but then we wouldn't be trying to destroy each other." I toyed with a ring on my right hand. A gift from Hunter on my last birthday. Parker gave me a matching necklace. I'd protested that I didn't need any shiny things, but in typical twin fashion, they insisted I deserved it. I didn't usually wear them, but after the last few months, I felt the need to have something from both of them close to me.

"Was teaming up to stay alive such a bad thing?" I asked. "Would you rather die than lose?"

Something flickered in her gaze. "You don't get it do you? I've done nothing but lose. I was born first, but I might as well not have been born at all. Dad always preferred you. Then our stepmother did. Our mother probably did too. Even Zachary…"

She scrunched up her mouth and shook her head. "Just once, I want to be first."

"Dad does not prefer me," I protested.

Although… I always got the impression he saw more of me in him than in Chloe. My stepmother used to help me with my maths homework, but Chloe never needed it. She was always better with numbers than I was. As for our mother, the memories of her were vague. If she had a preference, I couldn't remember, but I doubted she did. She was our mother, surely she wouldn't play favourites?

"Zachary cares about you," I told her. "You're all he wants. You're all Dane wants too."

"Both of them want power," she said bitterly. "They backed me because they knew they couldn't compete with the fucking Brantley twins. If you win, they'll hold so much power. Dane and Zachary would have had none."

She really was bitter.

"Dane and Zachary adore you," I said. "Yes, both of them want power, but they want you with it. Besides, I never would have had any interest in either of them. And vice versa. Dane has put everything on the line for you. He'd do it regardless of who you are."

She snorted in disbelief.

"Why don't you step aside from this competition and see?" I suggested. "Chances are, neither of them will walk away."

I wasn't completely certain of that. Dane, in particular, was desperate to claw back power for himself and his family. I doubted he'd go running to his cousin to do it. If that was an option, he would have already taken it.

Chloe laughed. "Good try. I'm not stepping aside

from this. I want Dad to look us both in the eyes and say I deserve to win. I want him to be proud of me." She pointed her perfectly manicured nail at my face. "Don't say he already is. We both know it will take more than what I've already done."

"This is about more than you winning," I accused. "This is about you seeing the expression on my face when I lose. You want me to— what? Cry?"

She leaned in closer. "I want you to do more than cry. I want you to know— I want everyone to know — I'm the better sister. When you lie awake at night, I want you to regret all the things you did that made people think you're better, smarter, more competent than me. All the things that got me overshadowed and pushed aside."

I frowned. "I never—"

"Yes," she hissed. "You did. Don't pretend you have no idea what I'm talking about. If I got an A, you had to get an A+. If I fell over and skinned my knee, you had to fall and break a bone. If Zachary fucked me, you had to fuck him too. If any guy looked at me, you had to get his attention. If it took me two tries to get my driver's license, it only took you one. If…"

I rolled my eyes. "You act as though sibling rivalry is something new. As if I'd break a bone on purpose." I narrowed my eyes. "If I remember right, I broke my wrist because you tripped me."

She sat back. "I wished I'd broken your neck."

Breathing the same air as her was becoming difficult. "There's still time."

She smiled slightly. "No way. Like I said, I want to see your face when I win. After that…"

"I hear the psychology faculty here at Brutham is very good," I said with forced evenness. "You might consider going to see them and getting some therapy." She was starting to make Zachary seem sane. Hell, she might give Ice Miller a run for his money in the unhinged department.

"You know what they say about revenge being the best therapy," she said.

"Revenge for what?" I asked. "For living my life? For trying to live up to Dad's expectations? For breaking a bone after you made me fall? Fuck that. I have nothing to be sorry for. Whatever picture you have painted in your mind, it's fucked up."

"It doesn't matter, I'm still going to win," she insisted. "You say you have no regrets now, but that will change. You will eventually. I promise you that."

Her cold fury knocked the air out of my lungs.

"I don't think you care about winning," I told her. "I don't think you really care one way or another if you lead the family. You have this idea in your head

—" I waved a hand in the direction of mine. "That somehow my existence is the reason why your life isn't perfect. If there was no competition between us, you'd make one. You would have done the things you did."

"Yes I would," she agreed. "Every bit of it."

I regarded her for a full minute or two. "I get it," I said softly. "You have nightmares about the rooms in the basement too, don't you?"

She shook her head faintly. "I don't know what you're—"

"Yes, you do," I kept my voice gentle but insistent. "Let me guess, he told you you needed to spend time in there because you weren't good enough at something." Her flinch told me everything I needed to know. "What was it?"

She averted her eyes. "You're wrong."

"No, I'm not. What did he tell you weren't good enough at?" I didn't expect her to tell me, but she needed to understand there was more to all of this. It wasn't about what I did. It was what Dad made her think about me and herself. Our whole lives were a mind fuck.

She scrunched her eyes closed like she was holding back tears. "He told me I needed to be better at everything than you, because I was the oldest. He told me I needed to think about what I'd

243

done and how I could do things better. He said time down there would give me the chance to think."

"But all it did was scare the shit out of you?" I guessed.

"I was weak," she whispered. "I let it get to me because I'm not as strong as you."

I stared at her in disbelief. "Is that what you think? You think I handled being down there better than you did?"

"Didn't you?" she asked. "Did you scream and cry and beg to be let out?"

I hesitated. "No. I curled up in a ball in the corner and hoped like hell he wouldn't forget I was down there." My eyes glazed as I thought back. The memories, the fear, were as fresh now as they were back then. I doubted they would ever disappear into a cloud of the past. They lingered too long and too close to the surface.

"After a while, I had myself convinced he had forgotten. I was sure I was going to die down there. Eventually, I thought dying might be easier than being in there any longer. I was ready to give up when finally the door opened."

"But you didn't give up," she said. "I did. I disappointed him and I disappointed myself. But I won't do that anymore." She wiped the tears from under her eyes with a vengeance. "I will never give up again. Even if one of us is dead at the end of this."

I sighed. "You realise we're messed up because of what Dad did to us? Right?"

"He only did what he did because he wanted us to be tough," she said. "I'll prove to all of you that I can be tough."

"By making my life miserable," I said.

"If that's what it takes," she agreed.

I frowned at her. A disturbing flash of under-standing popped into my brain. One I didn't want to contemplate too much, but I had to. Even if my stomach turned and my hands trembled.

"You're terrified that if you lose, he'll put you back down there?" The thought had occurred to me before. Judging by the way she shivered, it occurred to her too.

"If you win, he'll make you lock me in there," her voice wavered.

My blood went cold. "And if you win…"

She looked back at me for a solid minute before she stood and walked away.

The problem was, I wasn't sure if he had to make her lock me in one of those dark, unrelentingly miserable rooms. I would die before I let her do that to me.

I would kill.

CHAPTER 25

LILA

"Something makes me think we're not out here enjoying the sunshine," Parker said. He held my hand in one of his, while the other toyed at something in his pocket. I suspected it was the panties he stole from me the night before. While Slade was marking and Hunter was studying, he and I had a rare night alone. He'd made the most of it.

"Of course we are," I said lightly. "It's a beautiful day out here. The sun is shining. The kookaburras are laughing. I survived yesterday's exam. Why not step out and enjoy ourselves?"

Hunter raised his eyebrows at me. "It's not as though we don't appreciate your good mood, because we do. It's just that—"

"We've been worried about you," Slade finished

for him. "You've been quiet for the last while. Since the attack."

I shrugged. "I've been busy with essays and exams." I cocked my head at him. "Whose fault is that?" I smiled teasingly.

He grinned. "Brutham Academy. They tell us how many major assignments and exams we have to assign you. Ultimately that goes back to the school board."

"So it's all Reuben's fault," Parker concluded.

"Blaming him seems like as good a strategy as any," Hunter said. "And Lila's dad."

"If they don't kill us with mercenaries, they'll kill us with coursework," Parker groaned, a hand to his chest as though he was about to die under the pressure of study.

I frowned at the mention of my father but turned my attention to Slade. "Did you ever find any evidence that the school board endorsed that attack?"

"Not really." He draped an arm over my shoulders. "Either no one is talking or Reuben and Samuel did that all on their own. Of course, they contribute so much money to the Academy, the board can't kick them off."

"I don't get why Reuben and Samuel would work together," Hunter admitted. "What does Reuben have to gain?"

"Me dying?" I suggested. "Chloe and Zachary too. Getting rid of us would be guaranteed to make him smile. Even if you two were killed too."

"Chances were, Samuel wouldn't have been able to conduct his test without Reuben's backing," Slade said. "Reuben really had nothing to lose."

"Hey," Parker protested. "Hunter and I are not nothing."

Slade leaned over and patted his shoulder. "I know you're not. People like us are expendable to people like Reuben and Samuel, even if we're related by blood."

"You're not secretly a Brantley, are you?" I tilted my head back to look at him.

He chuckled. "Not that I know of. We're just brothers from different mothers."

"Sibling zoned," Parker looked slightly disappointed.

"Sorry dude," Slade told him. "I'm a one person guy and that person is Lila. For what it's worth, if I was going to screw another guy, it would be you."

That perked Parker up. "Thanks, dude. That means a lot. I always suspected I was hotter than Hunter, but this proves it once and for all."

Hunter barked a laugh. "Dream on, bro. You could wish to be as hot as me."

"All three of you are just as hot as each other," I

said firmly. I looked down the driveway at the sound of a truck rumbling towards us.

"What is this about?" Chloe demanded. She trotted down the steps out of the Academy, her phone in her hand. She must have made up with Zachary, because he was right behind her. Dane was nowhere to be seen.

"You know as much as I do," I told her. "Assuming you got the same text I did. Mine was from Dad, saying he had a gift for us for surviving his test."

"That's what mine said," she said carefully.

I shielded my eyes from the sun as a truck rolled into view. It came to a stop outside the building, maybe twenty metres away.

The driver opened the door and slipped out. "Chloe and Lila Bell?"

"That's us," I called back.

He grinned. "These are for you." He waved to the back of the truck where two brand-new Mercedes glimmered in the sun. One black, the other silver.

"Apparently they don't come in pink for Chloe." He shrugged.

"Good thing they had black," I said.

We stood back to watch as he drove the silver car off the back of the truck. He climbed out and handed the keys to Chloe before going back for the black one.

"This is very generous of Samuel," Zachary said carefully.

"Maybe he feels bad for almost killing us," Parker replied. "It seems like a couple of cars is the least he can do."

"Definitely," I agreed. It wasn't unusual for him to send extravagant gifts, but I doubted he'd ever done it out of guilt.

I accepted the key from the driver and toyed with it while he drove the truck away.

"Want to go for a ride?" Chloe asked Zachary. She dangled her key in front of his face.

Did she wonder what he thought about not getting a car himself? Honestly, he didn't seem too concerned. If anything, he seemed happy for her.

"Of course." He grinned. "I always want to ride you, and ride with you."

She batted his arm lightly, before unlocking her car and sliding inside.

"Drive carefully," I told her.

She rolled her eyes at me and slammed the door shut. The engine started with a purr. She gunned the engine, all but flying down the gravel, towards the road.

"Three… Two… One…" Parker said.

In the distance, tyres squealed, followed by a loud bang and the tearing of metal.

I leaned against Slade and exhaled softly.

"Oops."

Hi babes, Parker here. Thanks for reading our screwed up story. The steamy, probably fucked up conclusion to Brutal Academy comes in Vengeful. If you'd love a bonus scene, possibly featuring my bare ass, grab yours here.

If you loved this book and like to leave reviews, then get on your knees and write a review like a good girl.

ABOUT THE AUTHOR

Maggie Alabaster writes reverse harem romance.

She lives in NSW, Australia with one spouse, two daughters, one dog, and countless birds.

Jo Bradley writes contemporary romance.

Sign up for Maggie's newsletter! Sign Up!

Join Maggie's reader group! Join here!

Follow Maggie on Bookbub! Click here to follow me!

Check out Maggie's website- www.maggiealabaster.com

Sign up for Jo's newsletter

ALSO BY MAGGIE ALABASTER

Dusk Bay Demons

Puck Drop

Brutal Academy

Book 1 Heartless

Book 2 Cruel

Book 3 Vengeful

Court of Blood and Binding

Book 1 Song of Scent and Magic

Book 2 Crown of Mist and Heat

Book 3 Sword of Balm and Shadow

Book 4 Whisper of Frost and Flame

Dark Masque

Book 1 Bait

Book 2 Prey

Book 3 Trap

Saving Abbie

Book 1 Pitch

Book 2 Pound

Book 3 Session

Book 4 Muse

Book 5 Rhythm

Book 6 Encore

Novella Venomous

Saving Abbie books 1-4

Saving Abbie books 4-6 + Venomous

Ruthless Claws

Book 1 Ivory

Book 2 Crimson

Book 3 Elodie

Harmony's Magic

Book 1 Summoned by Fire

Book 2 Summoned by Fate

Book 3 Summoned by Desire

Shifter's Vault

Book 1 Discarded

Book 2 Deceived

Book 3 Disgraced

My Alien Mates

Book 1 Star Warriors

Book 2 Star Defenders

Book 3 Star Protectors

Academy of Modern Magic

Book 1 Digital Magic

Book 2 Virtual Magic

Book 3 Logical Magic

Complete Collection

Summer's Harem

Book 1: Shimmer

Book 2: Glimmer

Book 3: Flicker

Complete collection

Short reads

Taken by the Snowmen

Jingle All the Way

Also by Maggie Alabaster and Erin Yoshikawa

Caught by the Tide

Book 1–Pursued by Shadows

Book 2 Pursued by Darkness

Book 3 Pursued by Monsters

ALSO BY JO BRADLEY

Dusk Bay Sharks

Prequel Novella Sidelined

Spike

Punt

Intercept

Snap